BABBLING BROOK
SOCIETY

Marla —
    Watch out for Loggers!
Thank you for your support.

           Love,

i

Library of Congress Control Number:
2018966786
ISBN: 9781795412667

This book is a work of fiction.
Characters are a result of the author's
imagination.

Polar Caves Park and Quincy Bog are natural
attraction areas located in Rumney, New
Hampshire.

Karen Prescott

Dedicated to Stephen

Karen Prescott

Karen Prescott

CHAPTER 1

Luke unlocked the door to a familiar creak of floor boards, flicked a switch for overhead fans and welcomed a scent of old wood from the vaulted ceiling. He tossed his backpack in the office, pushed open the swinging door and greeted the fallow deer, pond ducks and geese with a cheerful hello before starting his hike through Polar Caves Park.

A cacophony of crickets and katydids made way for cicadas. Melodies from warblers and chickadees filled the air. Amid the chirps and birdsong, Luke could distinguish and identify tree frogs with their low, consistent trill. For this, he felt a tinge of pride.

He remembered second grade in elementary school. The nurse who administered a hearing exam explained what Luke should do. "You are going to hear some sounds. Every time you hear one, raise your hand or say, yes. Raise your hand as soon as you hear the sound, even if it's very soft. Do you understand?" He understood. His exam lasted longer than others who went before him. Upon completion, the nurse announced she needed to recalibrate the audiometer. She re-tested him.

When the second test was over she reported, "You have perfect hearing. Thank you." She smiled and waved to the next student. "Next." That was it. Perfect hearing.

The sounds of nature were calming. While at college, he listened to soft rainfall, ocean waves, or the crackle of a campfire with his headphones. Many nights he fell asleep to the sounds; any were preferable to the snoring of his roommate. Still, the digital version couldn't compare to actually being in the middle of New Hampshire. Here was better.

Strolling beneath the canopy of pine trees and maples, Luke smelled scents of pine and earth. He continued along Rock Garden, ascended to guide's platform, walked through the keyhole and climbed a stairway to Needle's Eye. He had memorized nearly every step and sometimes imagined that he walked exact footprints from his trek the previous day. He'd tread these cave trails many times alone and this was his favorite time of day, before any guests arrived. He was sure footed, like a mountain goat.

As Luke hiked, he thought about a recent proposal to his boss, Bob. He wanted to create a video to show on high definition monitors in the lodges. As a computer science major, he was skilled with technology and videography. His plan was to film the park with a head mounted camera, edit the video and add narration. Bob liked the idea and recognized the benefit for guests with limited mobility; they could watch a movie about the talus caves without having to make the hike. The sloping mass of rocks at the foot of a cliff wasn't the easiest to navigate.

After Bob gave his thumbs up, Gretchen became Luke's assistant. A creative writing major at college, she was ideally suited to write the script and her dramatic flair, honed from starring in theatrical performances, was fitting. To complete the project, Luke's duties would change slightly, but he would still do the job of safety inspector and be the first one through the caves each morning.

Luke liked being the proverbial early bird and as it happened, a bird's distinct sound brought the adage to his mind. A novice birder, he challenged himself to identify a bird's species or subspecies whenever possible. He saw a flier overhead, its wide wing span, bands of brown and white, a fan-like, striped tail. Those were the tell-tale signs of a hawk. He marveled at its majesty, its grace and skill; what a magnificent bird, he thought.

He watched it glide and circle. Swooping in Luke's direction, it flapped wings as if it wanting him to move along.

Curious, Luke stopped to watch it float on the wind and return with a loud screech. Was it heading towards him? It was!

Luke ducked as it dive-bombed. The hawk crashed into the back of his head, talons snatching some of his hair.

What the heck? Flustered, he waved his arms in defensive swipes.

The bird retreated, screeched again and pushed his wings to regain height. Luke snapped a photo of it circling a short distance away and lowered his smartphone when he saw the hawk start yet another approach.

Luke cautioned with arms outstretched, "Whoa!" He was prepared to defend himself now, but the hawk departed, its piercing whistle fading in the distance.

Rubbing the spot where it bashed him, Luke scanned the sky for other possible attackers. He looked out over the treetops and wondered. Was it pursuing or protecting?

Allowing himself time to recover from the encounter, he sat on the bench at Raven's Roost. Ever appreciative of the view, he looked across the Baker River Valley to the White Mountains and noticed Sandwich Mountain enveloped by a cloud.

He checked his smartphone for the photo. The image of the hawk was blurry, not clear enough to share on the Audubon Bird Guide app. He scrolled through photos online to identify its subspecies. It was a broad-winged.

Did they nest on rock ledges? No.

As he read about the characteristics of a broad-winged hawk, Luke heard an unusual, high-pitched noise. It seemed to be coming from a near-by cave named Bear's Den and sounded a bit like a moan.

Luke remained still as he considered the sound and supposed there must be a logical explanation for it. Perhaps the hawk's attack had rattled his ears and resulted in residual trauma, like a ringing of the ears or in this case, more of a squeaking. Perhaps it was an unusual bird call that just *seemed* to come from the cave. An echo?

Bear's Den was named by a staffer who discovered the cave. When he first entered it, he found a mama bear and two cubs. Alarmed, he shooed them away and luckily they ran out the other end. But, that was years ago and the sound was nothing like that of a bear. It was probably the muffled scream of a fox or a squirrel in distress.

He moved to the sound, descending the stairs into the cave, cautious as around a wolf's lair. He knew from experience that an injured animal should be approached with extreme caution, if at all. A quiet stillness pushed into every part of him. He waited and again heard a squeaky cry. It seemed to be coming from an opening in the cave wall, just a foot or so after the second lantern.

Pointing his smartphone flashlight into the dark crevice, its illumination revealed a small creature sitting on the rock floor. He was dressed in a red hat, gray coat and brown trousers.

"You're blinding me!" The little man screeched.

"What the...?" Luke retreated, falling back against the opposite cave wall.

Impossible! He drew in several deep breaths. Incredible! Luke doubted what he had seen. But, he quickly reasoned that he could and should, no, he *must* trust his hearing. He *had* heard the little man speak; of this he was certain.

Blinking hard and adjusting his eyes to refocus, he moved to the opening and pointed his light again. He noticed a shiny buckle and tools attached to the tiny man's leather belt. Intent to provoke a reaction, Luke drew a deep breath and blew as if extinguishing birthday candles.

"Why are you blowing at me?" the small man barked, holding both hands near his face for protection. The wee creature adjusted his blown cap, sent askew by the gust of air, and moved toward the intruder for closer inspection.

Luke's heartbeat accelerated and his hands shook when the small man moved in his direction. A strong urge to snap a photo for evidence, proof of this curious creature, moved his muscles to action. He fumbled with his phone and clumsily drop-tossed it, cringing when it slid down into a crack, its light bouncing off granite crystals.

The wee creature froze, uncertain about the object Luke had thrown into the crevice between them.

Luke squeezed his hand into the crack, but his phone was just beyond reach. Studying the situation to assess his best approach, he noticed something small and fuzzy on the granite floor beside the crevice. Luke lifted the furry object for a better look and admired the intricate detail of a tiny boot. It was fastened by a woven thread connecting the sole to its hairy sides; it was about the size of his fingernail with makings similar to a moccasin.

"Give me that! Ahhhh!" The little man lunged for his boot. Luke's fingers squeezed around it just before the determined creature landed on his closed hand.

Prying, digging, clawing at Luke's fingers, the tiny man's touch was prickly, tingling, almost like the beginning stages of frostbite. When Luke could reason that the wee man had no hope of opening his fist, he observed his determination with admiration. He was a courageous fellow. As the wee person struggled, his red cap flopped to and fro and bits of gray hair escaped from beneath its edges.

"Hey, just hold on!" Luke pleaded.

The tiny being stopped then and jumped off. He stood only five inches tall, hands on hips and legs apart with the unmistakable body language of anger.

Luke looked down at the little man. "I'll give it back, but first, tell me, who *are* you?"

"Willy Topper." He stood erect then, removed his hat and bowed with lavish formality.

The small man's sudden turnaround from frantic to formal surprised Luke. "Nice to meet you, Willy. I'm Luke." He opened his hand to reveal the boot, picked it up between his thumb and pointer fingers, and returned it.

Willy reached up for his boot and smiled. "Thank you," he said, before sitting on the rock floor to pull it on, grumbling about "too many acorn muffins and one too many goblets of lingonberry wine."

Luke watched Willy struggle to reach over his tummy, secure his boot and stomp it into position. He also saw the small man wince.

Luke asked, "Is your foot hurt?"

"It should be fine. I stubbed it. Serves me right for rushing. The bird..."

"The hawk?" Luke interrupted. "Was it here to get you?"

"Yes, *he* was."

Feeling at once pleased and proud to have saved the small person from an aggressive bird, Luke straightened his posture. "Well then, I'm glad I was here to protect you!"

"Protect me?" Willy was provoked. "He was my ride to the bog."

"To the bog?"

"Indeed."

"Quincy Bog? Is that where you're from?" Luke asked.

"No! I'm from here and I'd best be getting back. I wish a good day to you." He glared at Luke and appeared ready to remove his hat a final time to indicate his departure.

"Wait! Your boots are so..., uh, nice. What are they made from?" Luke's feeble attempt to engage Willy in conversation was a direct result of his utter shock and bewilderment. How was it possible for him to be conversing with this elfin being? A thousand questions percolated. He wanted to know *everything* about him.

He looked up and considered the Mort, a name Willy created to identify a human. Should he trust him?

Trusting a Mort was fiddly. Very tricky business. Not to be taken lightly.

Willy deliberated and waited for the signs. First, he listened to his inner voice. Next, he gave his heart a chance to settle. Finally, he waited for the feeling in his gut which would soon direct his thoughts one way or another.

He considered the facts: Luke found and returned his boot. He didn't appear hostile, having in no way attempted to injure or capture Willy. And, he *had* seen the tall, slender Mort around these parts before. Luke seemed trustworthy.

Amazed with the sight of this fairy, pixie, or elf, whatever he was, Luke studied the little man with golden eyes. Willy resembled an experienced miner, rough and rugged, but in miniature form. His tool belt, though somewhat hidden by his round belly, had tools for wood carving or rock chiseling, he guessed.

After many long minutes, Willy decided to give the Mort a chance and answered Luke's question about the composition of his boots. "Field mice hide."

Luke responded with a witty, "Well, do they?"

"Do they what?"

"Hide?"

9

"Who?"

"The field mice!"

Willy did not laugh, though he fully recognized Luke's attempt at humor. He tossed his head back and replied, "I dare say, I hope that you are not poking fun at my boots. If you are, I have a crew of five or so who could sail in the boats attached to those." He pointed at Luke's long feet.

Luke wore red and white sneakers, size 12. But use sneakers as flotation craft? He had never thought of that before. "Boats? Are you sailors?"

"Sakes alive! No, we are not sailors. And I'll wish you a good day!" Willy reasoned that he had been visible for longer than he should and wished to return to the safety of his cave home.

"But wait! Could you please help me get my phone?"

Willy stopped, obliged to assist. "Phone?" Is that what you call it?"

Quick as a spider, Willy scaled the granite, squeezed into the crack and used one of his tools to pry and maneuver the heavy, awkward object to just within Luke's reach. He stumbled back some distance when its light blinded him again. "Sakes alive! What makes it glow?"

Luke found the squeaky tone of his voice endearing. Initially, Luke thought the high pitch was from his anger or excitement, but now he realized it was his normal voice. Retrieving his phone, he turned off the flashlight and said, "Let me show you."

Luke held his phone upright to show the little man. Willy's gaze fixed upon the colorful icons.

The first icon Luke activated was Maps. A blue dot on the screen pulsed to show their location. "This is a map and this is where we are. See? Or, I can put in a location and it gives me directions."

Willy stood speechless, hands now in his pockets.

Luke reset the phone to his home screen and wondered what app to choose next. He picked Reddit. Its symbol was cute and in a way, reminded him of the miniature creature before him. "This is a gateway to news, stories, pictures, videos...," Luke waited as Willy studied the images and words. He scrolled through until it looked like Willy might faint.

Pressing the home button again, he touched his music icon. Luke said, "Listen to this."

"Don't Stop Believin'," played and Willy bounced his head, wiggled his shoulders and flapped his arms. When he moved his feet, he favored his injured foot, so Luke paused the music to show him something else.

"If I want to ask a question, I just say, "Okay Google, what will the weather be like today?"

His smartphone replied: "Today's forecast for Rumney is 85 degrees Fahrenheit and sunny. The forecasted high is 92. The low is 78."

Willy stepped back. "Are you joking? There's a girl named Google in there?"

"Just a woman's voice." Luke stopped then, having shown him perhaps too much. Luke had

11

had his lifetime to learn about computers and smart devices and now he feared what he'd shown Willy in such a short time overwhelmed the little guy. Luke said, "That's enough."

Willy stood now with his arms crossed resting on his belly. He studied Luke and the smartphone and shook his head from side to side. He paced. He leaned against the rock wall of the cave. Minutes passed. Willy seemed to have calmed, no longer interested in a speedy departure. He deliberated. Was his chance encounter with Luke a good sign?

Luke finally asked, "Are you okay?"

"Yes, if you would just give me a moment to think," he replied.

Luke thought that was rather odd. Willy had had many moments to think already. How long was a moment to a tiny person? Obviously longer than it was to Luke. Together they remained in the coolness of Bear's Den. The quiet between them gave Luke a chance to make sense of the magical occurrence of meeting Willy, who danced joyfully and thought deeply. Luke watched him remove and replace his bright red cap. He watched him stroke his beard and tilt his head.

Luke checked the time on his smartphone. He would be late getting back to the office, for sure. Not eager to rush Willy, yet anxious to hear what he had to say, Luke continued to wait and observe. Willy's eyes were distinctly different from humans. But, other than his sparkling, golden eyes, he resembled a tiny human with a scruffy beard, wrinkles and experienced hands. The gray coat he wore was slightly tattered. His belt reminded Luke of leather shoelaces on his Timberland boots and his shiny belt buckle appeared to have letters imprinted on it. Willy's cap was pointed and red, woven from fiber of some sort. It was hard to tell, but since it was the color of cranberries, he guessed they may have....

"Why is our ice melting?" Willy asked abruptly.

"Your ice?"

"Yes, the ice in the caves, it's disappearing. Can that thing tell me why?" He pointed to Luke's phone.

"Well, not really," Luke admitted, lifting and looking at it, unsure of how he would pose the question to his smart voice assistant.

Willy stood and adjusted his hat. "That's it for me then. I'll wish a fine day to you!"

"Wait!" Luke pleaded. "I mean, what I meant to say is that I can answer the question about the ice melting. I don't need to use my phone."

Willy looked up with such vigor and tilt, Luke feared he would topple over.

"Hmm. Let's see if I can explain this." Luke considered how best to respond. "Last summer was hotter than most, and dry too. We had very little rain. And, this summer, again, it's supposed to be hot and dry. Our weather patterns are changing and the scientists call it climate change. It's caused by too much greenhouse gas in our atmosphere."

Willy stroked his beard and replied, "I didn't know about the greenhouse problem."

"The gas is from burning fossil fuels, cars, volcanic eruptions, forest fires; all that combustion, well, it's causing a greenhouse effect," Luke explained. "It's like a greenhouse when it's warmed by the sun. If you don't let the heat out by opening a window, for example, the air becomes too hot. And that's what's happening. It's getting too hot. Icebergs are melting, so it's probable that your ice is disappearing for the same reason."

Willy shook his head and stared at the space between them. Luke knew his answer was only the tip of the iceberg, so to speak. He would need to be patient as Willy came to understand.

Luke offered, "Just tell me how I can help. You need ice, is that it?"

"Ice has been our water source. For generations, we have used deep Earth heated steam bursts to melt ice. With just the right amount of heat, we get just the right amount of flow. We control the water that comes to the community. The society relies on ice for the water to melt and babble, as we say."

"What society?"

"We are Toppers of the Babbling Brook Society."

"There's more of you? In there?" Luke pointed to the opening. "And you're called Toppers?"

"Yes, yes, and yes," Willy paused and nodded between each affirmative. He continued. "Your big caves lead to our small caves. We have homes deep in the mountain. I'm leader of the Toppers and that's why I came to the surface, to look for signs."

"Signs?"

"Indeed. Like you, Luke. If I can trust you, then you'll be a lucky sign, like a woodpecker, or a ladybug, or a rainbow. Signs are funny things. To some, the tendrils of a purple vetch are lucky. I guess it depends upon what things are around when good things happen. To me, even acorns are fortunate things. Perhaps I might regard you in similar fashion, Luke; you could be a lucky find. I could look to you for assistance, just as I did Charles."

"Charles?"

"I met Charles over and down there a bit," Willy pointed to the other end of the cave. "He was a helpful Mort, a very good friend, until he couldn't hear anymore."

"He lost his hearing?"

"Yes, sadly. When I called out to him, he passed along without even looking."

"Oh, that's sad."

"A very sad day, indeed." Willy agreed.

Luke paused to consider everything he'd just learned - a new world of little people and someone named Charles. "Tell me about Charles."

"He worked here, in the park," Willy replied.

"When?"

"That's hard for me to say. We don't measure time the way you do. But, the important thing is that Charles kept our friendship in strict confidence. We trusted him. I hope I can say the same for you, Luke. As the good book advises, "Only confide in tried friends, and never encourage idle curiosity." So, I wonder, Luke, can I trust you?" Willy stared at Luke with a serious expression.

"Yes, you can trust me!" Luke exclaimed, louder than he intended. "And, I'd like to help you get a fresh supply of ice, or at least water."

"Grand!" Willy squealed. "I accept your offer and will meet you here the next time you see a hawk." Willy bowed in a show of agreement and gratitude before disappearing into the crack that led to his hidden community.

It was time for Luke to move on; he'd been gone too long already. He hurried through the remaining caves, exited Smuggler's Cave and descended Mount Haycock.

When would the hawk appear again? Who was Charles? And more importantly, how could he help Willy with the ice shortage?

CHAPTER 2

Returning to the bustle of browsing visitors in Main Lodge, a typical day at the park was anything but ordinary for Luke. His mind reeled when he thought about his encounters with the hawk and Willy.

"Hey! That took longer than usual," said Bob, removing his National Caves Association ball cap. "How's it look up there?"

"Good," Luke replied, conscious of making his best effort to convey nothing unusual.

It was normal for Luke to linger and talk with Bob. They conversed about news, comparing what they learned from diverse delivery methods. Bob watched morning television shows, but Luke preferred online sources.

They stood abreast comparing stories while scanning visitor activity in Main Lodge. Bob did most of the talking because Luke's big news didn't come from Reddit or The Guardian this morning.

Beyond sharing stories in the news, Luke knew only a few other things about his boss. Bob had a Bachelor of Science in geology; he was passionate about all forces of nature and he was a sharp businessman.

Earlier in the season, Bob presented at a speleological event, sharing evidence of Native American artifacts found at Polar Caves. He called his talk *Cool Hiding Spots*. Luke offered to help him and had impressed Bob with his technical prowess and ability to transform a lack-luster talk into a dynamic, engaging presentation. It was well received at the conference and Bob knew he had Luke to thank, which he did. Bob wasn't technically savvy, but he appreciated people who were.

Though thirty years his junior, Luke was often left "in charge." If Bob had an errand to run or a meeting to attend, he trusted Luke to handle the business. Bob trusted Luke, but was the opposite true? Could Luke trust Bob? He knew that Bob would certainly want to know about his recent discovery and Luke felt obligated to tell him. These caves were a part of Bob's life, more than just a job. Perhaps he could hint about their existence and determine if Bob already knew about them. He could mention the little people, even if it was in a roundabout way.

Luke blurted, "There was... there was a..."

"Hold that thought," Bob interrupted, noticing a customer who waved him over, pointing into a display case. She wanted to see a necklace and another and another.

As Luke waited, the realization of meeting Willy Topper rattled him. How was it that Toppers actually existed? It was fascinating to think that a community of little people lived in the caves. This intrigue reminded him of a computer science lecture he'd attended about nanotechnology. He was amazed when he learned of scientists measuring nanoparticles, one-billionth of meter. It seemed unimaginable, but it was true; they were real. Just like Willy.

"You okay?" asked Bob, noticing Luke hadn't moved an inch and was staring into space. "Now what were you saying?"

"Er, ah... a hawk attacked me up there." Luke rubbed the spot on his head. "Ever heard of that before?"

"Hawks can be territorial, but usually only around their nests. Never heard of them nesting up there, so that is strange. Couple years back, I read an article about hawks dive-bombing people in Connecticut, so I guess they could be violent. Should you get checked out by a medical professional?"

"No, that's alright. Guess I'll get back to work on the video."

"You do that! We got more money wrapped up in video and computer equipment than we have in gift shop merchandise," Bob joked.

Luke had ordered a state of the art video camera equipped with an infrared sensor, shock and stabilizing mounts, lighting, cables, a tripod, a new graphics card, and another monitor. For Gretchen, his assistant, he ordered a digital audio workstation complete with audio interface, microphone and headphone. Bob was right. It was a substantial investment.

As he powered up his computer, he realized it was going to be hard for him to concentrate, but after a few clicks of his mouse, he started getting back on track. Soon he was viewing the footage of Bear's Den. Perhaps he could find clues or anomalies that might be connected to the Toppers. He didn't hear Dean enter the office.

"Howde do!" Dean announced.

"Hey there," Luke replied without looking up, fully absorbed in his work.

Dean grumbled to himself. Whenever Luke and Dean first saw each other or passed in the park, they fist bumped and exchanged: "You rock!" It was a better greeting than the standard hello, good morning or hey, and it was obviously appropriate for their location (caves twisting through granite crevices, a rock climbing wall, rock garden). Between them, it meant even more. They had a mutual love of performing and listening to classic, rock guitar (mostly 70's and 80's). They made time to jam at least once a week.

Dean resigned himself to non-compliance of their first bump routine. Luke was probably in a bad mood or maybe he just wasn't feeling well. No biggie. Friends didn't sweat the small stuff. He watched Luke's computer monitor from across the room. "Still a tad fidgety and dark, eh?"

"The wider lens helped, but it's still jumpy, even with the image stabilization. The luminous flux isn't right yet either." Luke leaned back in his chair and swiveled to consider Dean's response. There was none. Yup, Luke knew exactly how to throw out some technical jargon when he wanted to shake someone off.

Dean responded, "Ayuh. Give 'er another go." Dean took a long draw from the water he'd just taken from the refrigerator and added, "'Sposed to be a hot one today." When he was sure Luke didn't want to talk, he added, "Let me know if I can help," before turning to leave.

Luke was just about to respond with a customary thanks, but reconsidered. "Dean, hang on. Do you have a second?"

"For a fist bump? You betcha!"

Luke smiled and stood to pound his fist. "You rock!" Luke added a couple pats on Dean's shoulder to apologize for not fist bumping sooner. "Can you stay to talk for a bit?"

Never one to have to be asked twice, Dean pulled over a chair. "What's up?"

I just wondered, if, ah, if anything, ah, how can I put this?" Luke was flustered.

"Just spit it out," Dean prompted.

21

"I was wondering if you'd ever seen, I mean, if anyone reported, or...," Luke stopped. He took a deep breath and looked out a window to collect his thoughts.

Dean grew concerned.

Luke stammered again and finally asked, "Has anyone ever reported or seen anything that would be considered ah... unbelievable around here?"

"Unbelievable? Sure!" Dean's tone was one of relief and he quickly recalled just such an event, one that had baffled him over the years. "One summer, just before I started working here, a couple got married in Cave of Total Darkness. Written up in the newspaper and all. Just crazy! Are you thinkin' of puttin' that in the video?"

"No, not like that. I mean magical. You know, like sightings," Luke clarified.

"Well, no, not that I know of. I haven't seen any ghosts walking around, if that's what yer askin'."

"No, not ghosts. What about creatures? Any unusual creatures?"

"Creatures? Well..." Dean leaned back to think a bit before responding.

"There was a general manager who worked here, name of John. That was back in, geez, let me think..., 1965. Ayuh, I was in high school. John and his wife, Dot, got a family of baby racoons given to 'em. The 'coons were orphans, abandoned when the mom was killed. So John and Dot took 'em in and fed 'em baby formula. Only two kits survived. Kits. That's what you call a baby 'coon."

Luke nodded.

"Anyhow, they trained those two just like they were house pets! John and Dot named 'em Jayne and Mansfield on account of the fact that they'd seen a play with Jayne in it and they thought she was just fantastic. Ever heard of Jayne Mansfield?"

"Nope." Luke turned to his computer, swiftly typed her name into the search bar and displayed a photo of her.

"Wow, she *was* good lookin'!" Dean admired the photo of the voluptuous, blonde beauty. "She did summer stock around Lake Winnipesaukee. You ever been over there, to the Gilford Playhouse?"

"Not yet, but I heard it's pretty cool." Luke read from his computer and added, "Says here she died in a car accident."

"Tragic." Dean settled back into his chair before continuing with his anecdote.

"So, John and Dot loved those two 'coons. They brought 'em in the house to watch TV! John loved a good western. Anyhow, John used to fly an airplane for advertising; he pulled a banner that read: EXPLORE POLAR CAVES. And more than once, he took one of 'em flying with him. Jayne, I think it was. She loved to ride around in his car too. Those coons were like their babies. They taught 'em how to do tricks for the visitors. Ha! Those'd be some unusual creatures, eh? How they got wild coons domesticated, bringin' 'em into the living room to snuggle and takin' 'em up in the plane.

Gretchen should definitely write that one up for the video!"

"Thanks, Dean." Luke smiled and felt certain that if Dean knew of little people living in the caves, he would have mentioned it. "Guess we should get back to work then."

"Ayup. Replacing a few pieces of the boardwalk up at Tut's Tomb," Dean replied.

Talking with Dean calmed Luke and lifted some of the weight of keeping his secret. Luke told Willy he could trust him, but he also reasoned, if or when he ever told anyone about the Toppers, it would be Dean.

Dean had worked at Polar Caves for almost fifty years. Initially he was a guide, back in the day when guides would lead groups through the caves. He moved on to other positions and was head of grounds now. He liked keeping a close eye on any and everything. And Luke didn't mind one bit. Of all the workers, Dean was his favorite, always ready to help out or offer his two cents.

He was quite a talker too. He told stories about his experiences at the park. Crazy stories mixed with his New England dialect could crack a rib, that is to say, you laughed so hard it felt like your insides were busting. Some favorites were when he assisted hikers who got stuck in Orange Crush or Lemon Squeeze (easier said than done).

Dean was not only a great talker, he was a good listener, and Luke wasn't the only worker who sought his counsel. When Dean gave out advice it was usually one of his two favorite expressions: the golden rule of do unto others as you would have them do unto you, or say good things behind people's backs and say bad things to their faces. Many a work related conflict was resolved with the latter. Dean had earned the reputation of being straight-forward and sensible.

Resuming work on the video, Luke again looked closely at the footage of Bear's Den. He watched at regular speed and then slowed it. He could briefly see the opening where Willy Topper had exited. A flash of light, a sparkling glow just inside the crevice was visible. What was it? His video recorder light wouldn't have created that. He froze the image, reclined in his chair and stared at the mystical twinkle.

CHAPTER 3

Gretchen stored her lunch in the refrigerator and powered up computer equipment when she arrived. "Whatcha doin'?"

"Working on footage from Bear's Den," Luke replied, increasing the magnification of the curious flash of light. "What's this look like to you?" Luke pointed to the glow on his monitor.

"A lightning bug? What is it?"

"Not sure."

Gretchen sat and twirled in her chair as she spoke. "When I finish writing the script up to Fat Man's Misery, I was thinking we might have a bit of fun with the bypass for Devil's Turnpike, the Chicken's Walk. What if we superimposed animated chickens?"

She stood, flapped her arms and jerked her head, cackling, "Bok, bok, bok, bok. Whatdya think? I could do the sound effects if you did the animation."

Luke laughed at her playfulness. The fourth cave, aptly named the Devil's Turnpike, was a tough one. Sometimes your head practically touched your knees, the passage was so small. It extended 65 feet long and dropped 35 feet. "I'm going to have to say no to that."

She smiled, opening her spiral notebook to the section where she'd left off writing and recording yesterday: Mysterious Hanging Boulder. "Here's another idea. You know the Smuggler's Cave bypass, right? How about this? She made a sound resembling flatulence and giggled.

"Party Pooper's Lane. Very funny," Luke smirked.

"Seriously, though, I think there's more to discover when it comes to how the caves were used during Prohibition. I plan to check the local papers for anything about the Canadian whiskey bottles found in Smuggler's Cave. That would be interesting, don't you think? What if the Feds made an arrest?" Gretchen asked.

Luke agreed it might be worth looking into. Having worked together now for the past six weeks, Luke appreciated that Gretchen always came to work with a positive attitude and a spring in her step. She was fun to be around. He especially liked that she wasn't the type of girl who rambled on about reality television shows or celebrity break-ups or the latest nail art fashion.

When they stopped to talk, it was mostly work related; both were conscientious and focused on creating a top notch video.

"All quiet," Gretchen said, which meant she was ready to get to record. She cleared her throat and clicked her mouse to start.

"As you stand under this magnificent boulder, aptly named Mysterious Hanging Boulder, don't think about the fact that you are standing under approximately 60 tons of granite or the fact that this boulder rests on only three contact points from somewhere in the mountain. Chances are that it will never fall. Why? First, it hasn't budged in the last twenty thousand years. Second, earthquakes are extremely rare in this state. According to a state geologist from the New Hampshire Department of Environmental Services, the strongest earthquake with an epicenter in New Hampshire occurred at Tamworth on December 20 and 24, 1940, respectively, both with a measured magnitude of 5.8."

She paused, waiting for Luke's reaction before moving on to her third point. He responded, "If they're so rare, should you even mention it? And where is Tamworth anyway?"

"It adds that element of danger and thrill. But, you have a point. Let's find out where Tamworth is."

"I wouldn't say thrill, it's more like dread!" Luke typed Tamworth into his computer search engine. They looked closely at the map of New Hampshire and considered its proximity to Rumney. "It's less than an hour drive away," Luke figured.

"So? Should I leave it in then?" asked Gretchen.

"*That* is definitely a Bob question. If something happened here from the 1940 quake, he would probably know about it."

Gretchen found Bob at the gatehouse and asked about any recollection he might have pertaining to historic seismic activity in the vicinity, though very rare, the one that happened years ago, and would it be okay if she included a reference to the earthquake in her commentary?

He took in her whirlwind of information and thought about it for a moment before responding. "Lasted only a couple of minutes and shook things up a bit, but, no damage was reported here and those granite boulders haven't moved for thousands of years, so I doubt there's any risk. Best not to include it."

Gretchen redacted the earthquake language from her script and started that section over.

As Luke and Gretchen discussed how to present the Lemon Squeeze video segment, it occurred to Luke that he needed technology that would extend into a very narrow crevice. The Lemon Squeeze was only 14 inches wide and you had to enter sideways with your left foot and shoulder to get through. It was impossible to video it the way they did the other caves.

"How about a selfie stick?" Gretchen suggested.

"It has to be flexible to get around the bend."
Luke searched various sites on the Internet.
"Check it out, Gretchen. This one will be perfect.
It displays has a flexible scope, real-time video
with illumination and attaches a smartphone."
Luke would ask for Bob's approval before placing
the order.

Luke also needed Willy's approval. He already
had an idea about how to provide water for Willy
and it wasn't more ice. He would install a cistern -
a tank used for storing water, something he'd first
learned of while studying ancient Greece in middle
school. Water would come from rainfall or snow.
He planned on using plastic tubing to reach Willy's
home (though he wasn't sure where his home even
was) and it would need a control valve at the end.
Luke considered solar powered defrost panels or
mirrors to direct sunlight for warming in the colder
months.

When Luke determined the best position for the
cistern, he would need to secure it above Bear's Den
where it couldn't be seen. He doubted he'd be able
to do it alone; he would need help. This meant that
he needed to tell someone else about the Toppers,
but he wouldn't do that until he got the okay from
Willy.

After Luke helped Willy with his need for water,
he would ask if he could see his hidden cave home.
Luke's desire to see where Willy lived occupied his
thoughts. If he could send a video probe through

Lemon Squeeze, he should also be able to send it into the Topper community.

The video probe might just do the trick; he continued looking online and discovered a compatible extension cable, a necessary component if he sent the probe into the mountain. Just as cavers needed rope to navigate ascents and descents, he would need a long cord to explore the hidden cave.

Day after day, Luke and Gretchen worked together to produce the video with a little bit of laughter and a lot of serious, diligent effort. Luke walked the caves each morning, always stopping at Raven's Roost to listen and watch for a hawk. Each morning he started his route up with hope and anticipation and each morning he left disheartened. A week passed.

One afternoon, Luke took his lunch break on the porch of Maple Lodge. Most days he drove to Plain Jane's Diner or stayed in the office, but today he wanted to be outdoors. Maybe he could spot and identify a few birds. He munched on a peanut butter and marshmallow fluff sandwich. Not the best lunch, but he didn't have much variety at his apartment. As he sat looking across the Rock Garden, he heard the screech of a hawk, circling and floating. The bird!

Luke stowed his lunch and bolted, recalling Willy's last words: "Meet me here again when you see the bird."

Thankfully, no one else was in the cave when Luke entered. "Willy? Willy?" he called. Then, he waited.

He watched the hawk land on the railing just outside Bear's Den. As Luke sat motionless in the cave, he watched a glowing object leave the opening in the cave wall and quickly disappear out and up, onto the back of the bird. The bird immediately took flight. The glow was larger than a lightning bug but smaller than a bulb on a string of holiday lights, about the same sized light glow he saw on the video! Only two seconds passed from the time he saw a light glow and the hawk departed; it happened that quickly.

"Luke, hello! How are you?" Willy asked, standing on the edge of his cave entrance.

"I'm fine. I just saw a light glow jump on the back of the hawk!"

"That was Buddy. He's gone off to collect chokeberries."

"Chokeberries?"

"A bit tart, but we sweeten them with maple sap."

"But he was invisible!"

"That's what happens when we squeeze a star stone." Willy showed Luke an oval, dark stone with a center that resembled stars in the night sky. Rays of light erupted from its center. When Willy squeezed it, he transformed into a glow. Releasing his grasp, he reappeared. "We mine them here and polish them. Clever, don't you think?"

"Clever indeed." Luke paused to absorb the concept of little people turning into light glows when they squeezed a star stone. He continued. "I have an idea to help you with your water shortage, but I need the help of another person. I can't do it alone."

"Tell me more," said Willy.

Luke explained the cistern. When he finished, Willy approved. "It sounds like a good idea. But, who can you trust? Could you find Charles? It would be wonderful to see him again."

"The thing is, I don't know Charles."

"He's gone then?"

"I'd like to find him, but I'm not sure how."

"If you are secure in the confidence of whomever you tell, it sounds good to me. Thank you, Luke." Willy tipped his red cap.

Willy turned to go, but thought for a moment and said, "Wait. I have something for you." He returned with a trinket about the size of a thimble. "Ring this when you want to call me." He held up a miniature brass bell and jiggled it. "I made it for Charles, but never had the chance to give it to him."

"That's a tiny sound. I can hardly hear it," Luke replied.

"Well I can hear it just fine," Willy smiled.

Luke inspected the bell. It was made of thin brass with a miniscule loop on top. The bell was about the size of a pea, and it was hard to imagine that anyone could hear its sound further than a few inches away. He put the bell in his pocket and left

Bear's Den feeling better than he had in days. Luke headed in the direction of the deer pen where Dean was hammering a fence post.

CHAPTER 4

Dean was working on a wire fence he'd built thirty years prior, one he'd repaired or straightened many times before. The white-tailed deer liked to push up against the fence around their pen, especially if there was a hand full of corn on the other side.

He stopped, pulled his handkerchief from a back pocket of his worn jeans and swept his forehead. Like the alert deer, he sensed a change. They were frozen in place and when Dean looked up, he saw Luke's fast pace. He reminded Dean of an urban commuter running for a departing train and it certainly explained the reason for alarm. People didn't hurry at Polar Caves.

"You look like you're on a mission."

"Can we talk?" Luke asked, short of breath.

Never one to be pushed, Dean said, "Let me finish up this section and I'll come to the office."

"Actually, could we talk somewhere else?"

"Why? You got a secret?"

"Something like that."

"I knew it," Dean said smiling, shaking his head as if he had just been waiting for this all along, fully expecting it.

Luke was confused. "How do you know it?"

"I could tell."

"Tell what?"

"I knew you two were sweet for each other." Dean walked beside Luke and elbowed him, leaned in and muttered, "She's easy on the eyes, eh?"

"*What* are you talking about?"

"What are *you* talking about?" He stood aback.

"Look, Dean, I don't know what you think you know, but, I'm pretty sure you don't know what I'm about to tell you," Luke pleaded.

"So, it isn't about you and Gretchen?"

"No!"

"Okay, okay!" He picked up the box of nails and sledgehammer and pointed to extra fencing and a wire puller that lay several feet away. Motioning towards the tools, Luke understood his gestures and picked up the remaining items.

Dean surveyed the deer pen to make sure everything was picked up and in order. Together they walked to the maintenance building and returned tools to the workshop. Luke waited as Dean arranged his work bench, patient with Dean's meticulous and methodical "old-timer" ways.

"Take care of your tools and they'll take care of you." Dean reminded Luke of this as he waited. "Now, where would you like to have this talk?"

They sat in the gazebo named Serenity Shelter. Luke took a deep breath and began, "There are small people, tiny ones, only this big, living in the caves." He held up his fingers and measured about five inches.

Luke waited for Dean's response. There was none. Dean stared straight ahead. "Continue," he said, placing his elbows on his thighs and lowering his head to consider.

Luke stood. Dean's gaze followed. Luke looked directly into Dean's familiar, knowing eyes. "Continue? Does that mean you believe me? Because, not only do I need you to believe me, I need you to *help* me. This needs to be secret, too, completely and totally just between us."

"I believe you and you have my word," Dean assured him.

Luke returned to the bench and explained everything that he'd seen and heard, recounting his conversations with Willy Topper. Dean listened without interruption or comment. When Luke got to the part about the bird and a mysterious glow, Dean put his hand up.

"Hang on. You saw them glow?"

Luke nodded yes.

"Now, *that's* interestin'."

"It is?" It was Dean's turn to stand up. He took a few steps and pushed fingers through his gray hair. "Yup, I mean, the part about the glow and all. I heard something about a glow before."

"You did?"

"Ayuh, the first I heard of 'em was from my great granddad who heard it from his great granddad. Back, oh, gosh, now it was the late 1700's when folks were just settlin' in these parts. A lady, I can't recall her name, one of the early settlers, was travelin' horseback with her baby. She was headin' to Plymouth to meet up with her husband when it started gettin' dark. Now, mind you, in those days, a woman travelin' alone would need to protect herself from the Indians. Some were friendly, but not all of 'em. You just didn't know. Many didn't like the white folk comin' in and takin' over their land."

Luke responded, "Right. I'm familiar. We not only took their land, we spread diseases."

Dean stopped to consider the white man's impact. He continued. "So, when she saw night approachin', she knew she couldn't make it all the way to town. Left the horse tied to a tree down by the Baker River; the Pemigewassets used to call it the Asquamchumauke, and she and the babe headed up to Hawk's Cliff." Dean pointed in the direction of the cliff above Polar Caves and noticed visitors who were approaching the maintenance building. He would need to intercept them. "Hang on. I'll be right back."

Luke watched Dean introduce himself to a father and his teen boys. Dean was as considerate with visitors as he was with coworkers, nodding and pointing. He appeared to be making suggestions.

Dean returned and sat beside Luke. "It's good to see kids doing something other than playin' video games these days. It's good for them to be outside with nature. Got to talkin' about fishin' and suggested they head down to the Baker. Caught a 26 inch trout last weekend. Even told 'em the best lures to use. Now, where was I?"

"The woman traveling with her baby tied her horse down by the river. What was the name you called it?"

"Asquamchumauke. It means crooked water from high places. They renamed it Baker after he slaughtered them."

"What?" Luke was shocked to hear it. "Why?"

"Hard to say. If they were hostile, he might not have had another option. But, it's also possible the settlers were threatened by people who were different. I don't rightly know. But, my understandin' is that the river was renamed for him." Dean shook his head and stared at the ground, thoughtful.

"So, the woman tied her horse and headed to the caves," Luke encouraged.

Dean continued, "Now then, she told folk she saw little glows of light and the lights helped her find the caves. Her little boy pointed to 'em and made all sorts of fuss about the movin', glowin' objects and she took it as a sign to follow. The light glows led her into the caves where she spent the night with her son. The Pemigewassets never bothered her. They had a pow wow right above those X's on Hawk's Cliff and they never knew she was hidin' right beneath their noses. What if the glow you saw and the lights she followed were one in the same? Little people that lived in the caves?"

"That would mean they've been here a long time," Luke considered.

Dean continued. "The part about the light glows didn't make it to the history books. That part got passed on by word of mouth."

Luke stared in the direction of the Baker River and let his imagination roam to the days when farmers drove two-wheeled ox carts, men felled trees to build log cabins and people traveled on horseback. The country had just won its independence from England. Life back then was so much harder; survival was everything.

Luke continued. "Willy also asked me if Charles was still around. He said he worked here and he lost his hearing. Do you know who he was talking about?"

"The only Charles I knew worked here, oh geez, now, let me think, reckon it's been a good forty years now. But he could hear just fine. He wasn't deaf, at least not that I know of. That part I don't understand. You might check old personnel records."

"So, what do you think, Dean? Will you help me?"

"You know it!" Dean nudged Luke and they headed to the workshop.

As they hiked back, Luke said, "I really appreciate this Dean. It's a relief to be able to confide in someone. I've done some preliminary drawings. I could show you."

"Happy to help," Dean assured him. "I have a pretty good idea of what's layin' around here and we can build a cistern without any pictures. No offense."

"None taken," Luke laughed. This was definitely Dean's area of expertise. Dean prided himself in his frugality, his ability to pull together items, a direct result of his "pack rat" pride. You never know when you might need some thingamajig or another, he would say. Best not to throw it away if it could be used again. They entered the maintenance building and walked to Dean's tidy, cluttered workshop.

"Now, for the cistern, I'm thinking a sturdy plastic canister would work best. Light weight but dark, to absorb light in the colder months. I've got a twenty gallon over there, but since it's got to collect rainwater, we'll have to make holes in the top. Grab that drill and get busy."

"This size drill bit?" Luke held up the largest he could find.

"It'll have to do. I think I might have some tubing around here and I might even have a valve we can use. As for the solar power to melt ice in the winter, we'll have to do some research. Don't have any parts for that. Do we know where we're installing it?"

"Somewhere above Bear's Den. When we're ready, I have a way to signal him." Luke pulled out the tiny bell and struggled ring it. When it did sound, Dean couldn't hear it.

"What's that then?" Dean asked, when Luke hadn't finished his thought.

"A bell. Can you hear it?" Luke asked.

"Nope." Dean looked over for a glimpse of it. "Did you ring it? Wife says I may be hard of hearin'."

Luke returned the small bell to his pocket without extra thought and pulled out his phone. He should let Gretchen know his whereabouts.

He texted: **in workshop back soon**
Her response: **tyt** (take your time)

Luke drilled holes in the top of the barrel and cleared away bits of plastic shards. He rinsed the container under the industrial sink and as he watched the water coming from the tap, he wondered if Toppers would be drinking the water from this cistern. They shouldn't. He knew of all sorts of atmospheric contaminants that would be dangerous to ingest. He would need to explain this to Willy and if they did plan to drink it, he'd need to figure out how to make it potable. Did ancient Greeks have to worry about purifying their water? He wasn't sure, but two thousand years later, it was a concern.

Dean brought out fifty feet of plastic tubing and an angle valve. "Lookee here! Knew I saved this valve for a reason."

Luke watched Dean connect the valve to the tubing and the tubing to the barrel. After he returned the drill to its place on a shelf, he swept up the plastic shards. "It would be great if we could take it up there tomorrow morning. At sunrise?"

"I'll be there. First thing!" Dean assured.

Something occurred to Luke and he stood puzzling for a moment before he said, "Gretchen was looking through old pamphlets the other day and I noticed a mascot for Polar Caves. It was an elf with a pointed red cap. It reminds me of the hat, well, actually it's like the one that Willy wears. Any idea why?"

"Oh, that was back when I started working here. My dad used to tell me a story..."

"Hold that thought." Luke pulled out his smartphone.

He texted: **omw soon still in workshop**
Gretchen's response: **k**

"Go ahead, Dean. I'm all ears."

Dean took a seat in his brown leather office chair, worn and ripped in obvious places. Black duct tape held stuffing inside. Some brass grommets were missing and if the leather wasn't covered with tape, it was cracked. The chair was the most comfortable place in the shed, and it was Dean's. No one else sat in it. Ever.

"So, this miner liked to come to the caves, I'd say it was in the early 1900's, before Collishaw turned 'em into a spot for tourists. The miner was searching for beryl. You can find emerald and gold crystals in the granite deposits. Fetch a decent price, too. A real *spelunker* he was..." Dean waited for Luke's reaction.

"Spelunker?" Luke smiled. Dean emphasized the term used for a cave explorer as if to impress. But he didn't need to. Luke knew it took more than formal schooling to gain wisdom. Dean started working at Polar Caves immediately after graduating from high school. It may have been the end of his official education, but it didn't matter. Dean was one of the smartest people Luke knew.

Dean continued. "Anyway, it was a hot summer day and no better spot to explore, mine and keep cool at the same time. He fell asleep in one of the caves or just lost track of time. The sun set and his oil lamp ran out. It got dark and he knew his family would be worried, so he started getting' nervous. Yellin' wouldn't help. Who's gonna hear him from the caves, right?"

Luke agreed.

"The way he told the story is that cave elves helped him. He followed the small creatures until he could make it safely out to Route 25. When he got home, he told his family about how he was helped by the pixies and that's how he described 'em, with red caps and funny boots. The story passed around and the image stuck."

Luke wondered, "You got any other stories about elves?"

"I could make some up!" He laughed. But, after a moment of levity between them, Dean grew thoughtful. "You know, Luke, I've been thinking about these little cave dwellers and it seems to me that something has changed."

"How so?"

"In the past, the little folk have always been the ones to help us. Now, we're the ones helpin' them."

CHAPTER 5

Luke usually didn't have trouble falling asleep, but last night his mind raced. How and where would they install the cistern? Would the water be clean enough? How would they melt snow and ice in the winter months? He remembered checking the clock at 3 A.M. Seriously needing some shut eye, he tried using relaxation techniques to visualize billowy clouds floating through a blue sky. That helped until a hawk appeared and startled him awake.

He rolled over to stop his alarm at 4:30 A.M. It would take him ten minutes to get ready, fifteen minutes to get to the park and another five minutes to get up to Bear's Den. He pushed his long, slender legs into cargo shorts, pulled a fresh shirt over his head, placed the miniature brass bell in his front pocket, slid his phone in a side pocket, grabbed an energy drink, a granola bar, and hopped in his car.

Dean was waiting for him inside the workshop. "You okay? You look tired." Luke returned a groan.

Dean laughed and slapped him on the back. "Give it up!" Dean prompted him for their fist bump. "You rock!"

No matter how out-of-sorts Luke was, Dean had a way of making him feel better. Dean checked his watch and reported, "Ten minutes to sunup. Stand still." Luke obeyed as Dean looped plastic tubing around his neck. "How about that for a necklace?"

"Very funny," Luke chuckled. He lifted two large jugs of water, one in each hand. Dean attached his tool belt and lifted the cistern. Up they walked with their loads.

Luke stood just outside the cave, pinched the top of the bell and shook once and twice. He waited near the entrance as Dean looked out across the valley from Raven's Roost.

Willy appeared. "Good morning!" He stretched his arms over his head and bent at his waist to touch his toes, reaching, reaching and giving it a good try before giving up and standing upright with hands on hips. "This is an early surprise visit!"

"We're here to install the cistern, but first, let me introduce you to Dean." Luke waved his arm toward Dean and Willy hopped on a nearby rock for a better view.

Dean gasped when he saw the tiny man. All these years working at the park and this was his first time meeting the tiny cave dweller! The sight of the small creature stopped him in his tracks. He wobbled, bent over for a closer look and shook his head in disbelief. Dean was rarely tongue tied, but he was speechless now. Unable to collect his thoughts or muster any words, he stood, mouth agape, entranced by the little man.

Luke watched Dean's reaction with delight.

Finally, Dean sputtered, "Howdy do, sir?"

Willy responded, "Very fine indeed and pleased to meet your acquaintance!" He removed his hat, swept it beside him and bowed for the introduction.

Dean stared at Willy and asked, "Did you just say somethin'?"

Luke replied, "Yes, couldn't you hear him?"

"Nope," confirmed Dean.

"He can't hear you, Willy."

"He's deaf?" wondered the little man.

"He can hear, Willy. He just can't hear *you*."

"That is curious; I am able to hear him," Willy confirmed.

Luke scrunched his brows. Was he the only one who could hear Willy?

"Well, let's get this started. We don't have much time," prompted Dean. "At least I got to see the wee lad."

"Did he just refer to me as a lad? I'm certainly older than him! A lad? Humph." He crossed his arms, clearly offended. Dean watched him with a quizzical expression, not sure why he looked irritated.

To divert Willy's annoyance, Luke said, "Before we get to work, could I capture your voice on my smartphone, Willy? It'll only take a second." Luke held his phone in front of him.

"Do you mean like the Google voice?"

"Something like that, yes."

"What should I say?" asked Willy.

"Anything," replied Luke, activating his recording feature and nodding to indicate Willy should speak into his smartphone.

Willy responded, with a slow, systematic pronunciation, "An-y-thing."

Luke chuckled; he would need to be satisfied with that for now.

"Up we go!" said Willy who scooted up and over the rocks. He made it look so easy, like a gecko with sticky toe pads.

Dean studied the terrain above. "Don't think I'll be climbin' up there," he defended. "Besides, it's against park rules."

Luke struggled to climb the boulders after Willy, sliding in his attempts to gain a sturdy foothold. Dean offered him a boost and encouragement.

Willy watched from the spot where they would guide tubing into the community. "This opening leads to our ice reserves or what used to be, I should say," he explained. Luke peered down into the dark hole.

Their challenge was to locate an acceptable spot for the cistern. Dean directed as best he could from the platform, passing materials, tools and advice, instructing Luke to hammer this against that and use this gizmo to wedge that over there. Finally, their efforts resulted in a secure placement for the container and from Dean's perspective, it was hardly noticeable.

Luke pulled jugs of water up and explained to Willy, "I'll put just a small amount of water in the cistern at first. After you have the tubing and valve in place, I'll put in the rest. I don't want there to be too much initial water pressure."

"Not to worry, Luke. The gents and I will be able to handle the flow with controls we've developed over time. You just fill it right up! When we finish, I'll be back up to give you a report."

Luke watched Willy's technique for getting down from the rocky ledge. He held fast to a fern and slowly released his grip, slid down swatches of lichen and landed on the various jutting rocks. What worked for Willy wouldn't necessarily work for him, though.

"He makes it look easy," thought Luke. He just wanted to make it down without breaking a bone.

Luke made himself as comfortable as possible, given his awkward position atop granite boulders. After he emptied the jugs, he tossed them onto the walkway below.

"I best be gettin' back," said Dean, gathering the jugs. "Bob'll wonder where I am. Careful gettin' down."

As Luke waited, he listened. Leaning toward the opening he thought he could hear voices below. His heartbeat quickened at the thought of a community of Toppers. He was curious to know everything about them and eager to send a video probe down to view their world. Did it receive sunlight? How big was it?

He was also anxious to experiment with the recording he took of Willy's voice, curious whether others would be able to hear it. What if he was the only one who could hear Willy?

Luke was grateful for the view. It was another glorious day in New Hampshire. A bird would glide past occasionally and he challenged himself to name the species. It would take years of studying and observing before he considered himself a real birder, but with anything, it got easier the more you practiced. He kept his field guide handy and studied it whenever he got the chance.

"Swallow." He watched the bird fly to a nest on the cliff where it landed in a sheltered nook. It twittered, as if to say, "I'm home." Luke heard squeaky chatter in response, but couldn't tell from where it came. Another bird flew past. "Blue jay," he said aloud. Looking out over the treetops, he saw another and made a mental note of its characteristics: yellow, small, black and white wings.

Willy appeared at the cave entrance below and yelled up to Luke. "We're all set!"

Luke lowered himself to the walkway with only a few scratches and no broken anything. What a relief. He stooped to follow Willy into the cave and waddled until he found a comfortable spot. Their eyes nearly level, he had a good view of Willy. Luke had many questions, but decided to start with one that especially puzzled him. "How do you get hawks to transport you?"

"We whistle."

"You can imitate their whistles?"

"Yes. They hear our call and nearly always arrive."

"Have you always done that? Used a hawk to catch a ride?"

"No, previously, we rode ducks, but then they, well, I guess one might say they got wacky."

"Wacky?"

"Yes, their crazy behavior was a direct result of eating the white stuff. We switched to hawks and have found them to be much more reliable."

"What's the white stuff?"

"Most of it is white so that's what we call it. It's food Morts throw to them. Mostly pieces of white bread, sometimes crackers. Morts throw chunks of white stuff to them and they slurp up the gooey mess. It's disgraceful. They go bonkers, get loopy. Instead of eating what they should be eating: weeds and bugs, they've become lazy. And the more white stuff they eat, the more they want, traveling to those spots where Morts are most likely to toss it to them. It's wreaking havoc on their brains and there is no telling what it's doing to their bodies!"

"But we only have corn for them here at the park,"

"Corn is okay, but that's only the half of it. Morts still throw the white stuff. I've seen it happen."

"How do you talk to the ducks?"

"Why we, kwan, quack, like that." Willy imitated the sound of a duck for Luke and it sounded amazingly similar, really just like a duck.

"And they understand you?"

"Our communication with them is limited only because their vocabulary is limited. Hawks are smarter, so it's been a better arrangement all around."

Luke considered what he'd learned before posing his next questions. "How have you learned? Do you have schools?"

"We learned from books given to us by Charles. First we needed to learn your language. Charles brought the English language and the books into our community. We started with *Grammar of the English Language.*"

"But how can you possibly get a book down there?"

"We have miniature books, just the right size for us. He gave us *Robert's Rules of Order*, and *The Handbook of Etiquette: Being A Complete Guide to the Usages of Polite Society*, which I have read so often, I am able to recite. Shall I?"

"Yes, by all means," Luke encouraged.

Willy cleared his throat and proceeded, "In order to enjoy polite society, and to be thoroughly suited for it, we must have a knowledge of those rules and regulations which the custom and common consent of well-bred people have established and drawn up into a kind of social code, entitled Etiquette."

Willy grinned and straightened his posture, entirely pleased with himself.

"That's the book you quoted before, about friends and idle curiosity?" asked Luke.

"The handbook about etiquette, yes. Charles impressed upon us the importance of good manners. He would often quote famous writers. Perhaps you would know to whom we may credit this?" Willy held his arm across his chest as if to honor the statement. "Life be not so short but that there is always time for courtesy."

Luke repeated the sentence aloud, reciting to commit it to memory. "Hmm, I'm not familiar with that one. I'll have to check on it."

Willy continued. "Another excellent book has taught us the basics of science: *Principles of General Science*. If you should ever find Charles, perhaps you could ask him if he might obtain additional books? We could use new ones, though, I will say that reading Dickens or Tolkien more than once is never tiresome!"

"You've read Dickens and Tolkien?" Luke was shocked. "Have you read *The Hobbit*?"

"Excellent story! I like to think I may be related to Bilbo Baggins."

"Are all little people called Toppers?"

"Oh no, there are Boggers and Loggers, too. Loggers are a tad fussy, but we get along famously with the Boggers! Speaking of Boggers, may I ask a favor of you?"

"Just say it," Luke assured.

"We are in need of bog plants. We use them to purify the water, you see."

"I was wondering about that. You purify with plants?"

"Yes, and other filtration methods we've perfected over time. The water travels over a system of rocks and pebbles, moss and plants before arriving in our pond. It's precisely why we call ourselves Babbling Brook Society. We pride ourselves in pure, clean water. Most important, don't you think?"

Luke agreed.

Willy continued. "Use the bell I gave you to alert Barbara Bogger; she'll supply the plants we need. I'll send a star stone as trade."

"How will I know where to find Barbara?"

"She's at the bog. You know it as Quincy Bog. But you bring up a fair point. It would be difficult for me to give you directions as I can only describe the location from a bird's eye view. No worries. We'll signal hawks for transport when they return from their pre-migratory meeting. Just thought I might speed things along."

The bird's eye view gave Luke an idea. "Wait. I might be able to help." He activated Google Earth on his smartphone. "I'll pull up a satellite view and you can show me their location."

"Satellite?"

"A satellite is a piece of technology that revolves around the Earth. It's like a camera high in the sky, the same view that you'd have if you were riding on the back of a hawk."

Luke spoke into his smartphone. "Rumney, New Hampshire." They waited for a map to load. Using his fingers to zoom out, he showed Willy.

They studied the image. Willy pointed to the upper right quadrant and asked, "Can you make that bigger?" A small mound of earth about twenty feet from a man-made bridge became visible. "That's it! Right next to the bridge, there." When Willy touched the screen, it flashed, popped and went dark. Luke saw a spark jump between Willy's finger and the screen.

"What happened?" Luke gasped.

Willy said, "You were touching it, so I thought I could too."

"I know. I know. Oh, man."

"Is it broken?" Willy asked as he watched Luke press buttons on the front and sides, shake it and press the same buttons again. When nothing worked, Willy said, "I'm sorry, Luke."

"Oh, man."

"But, did you see the spot I pointed to?"

"I think so."

"That's where you'll find Barbara. Wait here while I get a star stone."

"Sure...." Luke was distraught. He was still holding down the power button and waiting, hoping for it to start, shaking off his disbelief when Willy returned with the stone.

"Are you okay, Luke?"

"I guess. It's just that I was going to experiment with that recording you did and I have all these recent pictures and..."

"I'm very sorry," Willy repeated.

"I don't understand what happened. Why would the touch of your finger fry my phone?"

"It might have something to do with our power, the same power that works a star stone. Here you go," Willy handed the stone to Luke.

Luke admired the small stone. The depth of dark colors, black, blue, green shades and light specks captivated him. "Wow, this is cool. Okay, Willy, I'll see you again with the plants. And you're sure Barbara will hear the bell?"

"Positive. Just ring it a few times when you get to the bog spot and she'll know I sent you. When you can hear the trickle of a waterfall, you're close. Thank you!" Willy scooted away.

Luke walked the trails, his thoughts whirling. He never saw a phone do anything like that before. Immersed in water, sure, it would short-circuit, but flash and die like that? Never.

Luke entered the office, sullen and confused. Before he could edit any video footage, he wanted to search problems with his model of smartphone. He noted very few difficulties logged by users and none that resembled what just happened. Out of sheer frustration he typed: **super-charged cave elf blows up smartphone**. No results. No surprise, either.

It must have been the energy surge coming from Willy. He understood the capacitance needed to work a smartphone, a human touch on the screen sent just the right amount of electrical impulse to activate points and swipes. If Willy had more electrical charge coming from him, it might explain how he cooked Luke's device.

Dean arrived shortly after Luke. "How'd it go?"

"Good and not so good."

"Explain," he replied, taking a seat to listen. Luke recounted most of what happened earlier that morning. The little people were set. The cistern above the cave worked and now they'd have a supply of water. Willy fried his phone; it wouldn't even turn on. He had to meet up with Barbara; he would go at lunchtime. Whew! It had been quite a day and it was only 9:00 in the morning.

What Luke didn't know was that Gretchen stood just outside the office door listening to their entire conversation.

CHAPTER 6

Gretchen leaned on a wall outside the office door. She heard the familiar creak of a chair and knew Dean was on the move, probably headed in her direction. She bolted to a restroom and closed the door behind her, stared at her reflection in the mirror and questioned what she had just heard. *Are little people really living in the caves?*

She ran water over her hands. *The little people now had a supply of water.* When the faucet stopped running, she shook off the excess and covered her face with damp, cool hands, thinking of mysteries within the hidden depths of the caves. Needing time to collect her thoughts, she pulled out her hair elastic releasing shoulder length, wavy, cinnamon hair. She shook her head, gathered and again secured her customary hairstyle, a ponytail.

Stalling for time, she pulled her phone from the back pocket of her shorts, more for distraction than necessity. *Willy fried Luke's phone.* Who was Willy? She shoved her phone back into her pocket.

Returning her attention to the mirror, she leaned in to check her makeup. Gretchen had hazel eyes, accentuated with eye shadow, just the right color, not too much. Did Luke even notice her eyes? *He was going to meet Barbara at lunch time.* That bothered her more than she wanted to admit. Self-control. Just keep it cool, she told herself, leaving the bathroom.

Gretchen entered the office with her usual, cheerful, "Good morning!"

Luke returned a gloomy, "Hey."

"Why so down?"

"My phone is dead."

"What happened?" Gretchen moved closer to see.

Luke pried the battery out to inspect its condition. He muttered, "Yeah, it's cooked."

"Don't you have insurance?"

"I do, but you know, it's just the hassle of replacing everything."

She understood completely and decided changing the subject was probably best. "I'm ready to start on Smuggler's Cave today. Then, I'll record the audio for Lemon Squeeze. Sound okay?"

"No rush on that. I won't be able to use the video probe when it arrives. It has to connect to my smartphone." He took a deep breath and used his computer to familiarize himself with Quincy Bog. After that search, he focused on the footage of nature trails which still needed editing. Both of them worked for hours, conferring when necessary. Gretchen was careful not to interrupt Luke too often. But, every now and again, she needed to chat.

Gretchen asked, "Have you ever been to Rumney Rocks?"

"No," responded Luke, "Have you?"

"No, but I'd like to go sometime," Gretchen said with a hopeful tone.

Luke resumed work on his computer. Gretchen wrote and edited the script until it was almost time for their lunch break.

Gretchen asked, "Did you hear that Jason Mraz is playing at the Pavilion on Friday?"

"No."

"Do you like him?" she wondered.

"I do." Luke welcomed her suggestion and typed amphitheater Lake Winnipesa... and stopped to let Google finish the spelling for him. "Let's see if there are tickets."

Minutes later they were choosing their seats.

Gretchen's heart leaped. It would be their first date. Quickly, her thoughts turned to Barbara. She didn't want them to, but as thoughts often do, they emerged. Pesky things.

She blurted, "Won't Barbara mind?" Her tone was harsh, cutting. Had she really just said that? She immediately wished she could take it back. It was as if a devil spirit had taken control of her tongue and forced it out. His reaction confirmed her dread.

"What did you just say?" Luke shot a look at her. "How do you know about Barbara?" He glared as she contorted her mouth and scrunched her eyes.

"I was sort of eavesdropping. I know you have a lunch date with her. I just wondered..."

Luke stood up, walked to the office door, looked outside to see if anyone was nearby or likely to enter and returned. He stood at least six inches taller than her which was usually no big deal, but now he seemed to hover.

"What else did you hear?" he asked.

"Everything."

"*Everything?*"

"At first, I didn't want to interrupt and thought you were just talking about work, but then, I couldn't believe what I was hearing and... and... I couldn't pull myself away. Is it true? Are little people living in the caves? You can trust me, Luke. I won't tell a soul, I promise."

Luke took a deep breath, resigned to the fact that she knew and more thankful than angry that she had overheard. "It's true. Willy Topper is the leader and I've spoken with him twice. Barbara is the leader of the Boggers and she's the one I have to find today. It's not a date."

Relief swept across Gretchen's face. "Oh! So, she's a little person too?" Luke nodded yes, staring directly into her beautiful eyes. Their gaze held.

Gretchen asked, "How is it possible, Luke?"

"I know, it's hard to believe. It's taken me days to process this. But, it's true. They exist."

She asked, "Can I go with you, to meet Barbara?"

"I think it's better if I go alone. But, you could help me find a guy who worked here about forty years ago. His name was Charles. Could you check the old personnel files?"

"I'm on it," assured Gretchen. "How will you carry the plants that Barbara gives you?"

Luke hadn't thought of that and Gretchen figured as much. She opened her insulated lunch bag, removed a plastic, resealable sandwich bag containing zucchini strips and halved radishes, and dumped the vegetables onto napkins she had placed on her desk. "Take this," she offered, holding out the clear bag.

Luke accepted it and shoved it in his left shorts pocket with the star stone. He touched his other pocket to check for the tiny brass bell and looked down at his smartphone.

"Do you want to borrow my phone?" Gretchen offered.

"I'll manage. Thanks anyway."

"Good luck," she said with a kindhearted smile.

There was so much Luke wanted to say to her at that moment, but the urgency of the mission trumped his desire to tell her that he trusted her and was relieved she knew.

He drove about four miles before he saw the sign on Route 25 for Quincy Bog Natural Area. He was half way there when it came to driving distance, yet if he were a hawk, it would have been only a mile away. As the crow flies, they say.

Once he reached the parking area there would be a trail map to guide him. All he had to do was look for the bridge, head off-trail along the water's edge and listen for a small waterfall.

Earlier in the office he'd had just a few moments to read up about the area and learned that though most people referred to it as a bog, technically it was a low, marshy area called a fen and was formed around the same time as the caves were, at the end of the Ice Age. He wondered if Boggers and Toppers were as old? Fifteen thousand, twenty thousand years? It was hard to imagine. He recalled Willy saying they measured time differently.

He turned onto Quincy Bog Road and parked his car. Relieved to see no other cars, he consulted the kiosk for direction. He would take a right on the path located a short distance before him.

The path was well worn, covered with pine needles and planks of wood over muddy areas. Bracken and wood ferns dotted the landscape. It was peaceful, the water calm, the birds sending bursts of song now and again. The bridge was easy to spot.

Luke walked to the center of it, looked out over the waveless water and spotted a beaver dam. Those engineers of nature, the incredible, busy beavers; he marveled at their ability to alter the ecosystem. He wished Gretchen was with him to appreciate the peace, the tranquility, and the view.

He turned around and recognized a portion of land jutting into the pond. This was the spot. Returning to water's edge, he walked along bog shrubs until he could hear the soft dribble of a waterfall. He scanned his surroundings, looking left and right. He was alone.

Lifting the tiny bell from his pocket, he squeezed the loop at the top and rang it. Such a miniscule sound, the tiny bell reminded him of *Peter Pan*, a favorite story from his childhood. The tinkle of bells was fairy language, Peter had explained to Wendy, and whenever a child somewhere said they didn't believe in fairies, a fairy died. Luke wondered if Barbara might resemble a fairy.

Luke rang it again and waited. He leaned against a tree and concluded that Toppers and Boggers were never rushed. He rang the bell a third time, and held it beside his ear, only an inch away, to better hear.

Birds caught his attention. "Warblers," he said. He heard their noisy chirps and watched them perch.

He saw purple flowers sticking up from the water and guessed he spotted a beaver in the distance, skimming along the water surface. The surroundings had a peaceful effect and he sat beside the tree realizing how tired he was.

He felt himself nodding off. What may have been seconds or minutes later, a shrill sound startled him.

A sweet, screechy voiced called out. "You hoo!"

Across the water he saw the small creature standing on a clump of bog grass, waving her hands and calling out "Over here!" Her call was not particularly loud and it was very high-pitched.

Luke approached Barbara Bogger, his eyes fixed on her dark green, oversized chest waders. They reminded him of a pair his grandfather wore when fishing. He remember his grandpa referred to them as his "Wellingtons." The waders would keep her dry, Luke thought.

She had the coloring of a bullfrog and the sound of a screech owl. And when she waved her arms, encouraging him to move in her direction, calling out again, "You hoo! You hoo!" he worried that she might fall into the pond.

He was compelled to respond. "Coming!"

As he approached, he thought the waders looked more like the skin of an amphibian, a snake perhaps. How clever! He also noticed her decorative headpiece made of yellow feathers. Warbler perhaps? Her clothing was unusual, that was for sure.

Navigating the uneven ground beside the water's edge and totally captivated at the sight of this curious miniature, he tripped and fell into the mucky water, sending the tiny bell flying with a kerplunk.

Barbara yelled, "Oh no! The bell!"

It was difficult for him to extract his left arm from the peat bottom of the pond and in trying to keep some part of him dry, he succeeded in getting more of himself wet. When he finally cleared his way from the muck bottom, he tried his best to wash the mud from his arms and legs.

Luke couldn't hope for one moment that he would ever find the bell. Silt clouded the water and the bottom would have swallowed the bell in the same way it wanted to swallow him, had he not exerted considerable effort in resisting its suction.

Barbara Bogger stood shaking her head. Upon closer inspection, her yellow head feathers were attached to a band of some sort. In her hand, she held what looked to be a weapon, a sharpened tooth from a mammal or fish. He couldn't be sure of its origin, but he was positive she was pointing it at him.

"Right. Now, who might you be?" asked Barbara.

"I'm Luke. Willy sent me."

"He did, did he?" she mused, waving her weapon about in a circular motion.

"I'm here to get water plants from you. He said you'd know what he meant and sent a star stone for trade." Luke reached into his pocket for the stone and pulled out the bag Gretchen had provided.

When Barbara saw the plastic bag, she shrieked and shielded her eyes. "Ahhh! Take it away!"

Luke quickly shoved the bag back into his pocket. From her reaction, he thought it might have the power to inflict pain or injury or, perhaps she was allergic to it? "I'm sorry!" he exclaimed.

Barbara held the weapon in attack position, her tiny white knuckles tight around it. Her round, golden eyes raged. Her body was in a fighting stance.

She blasted, "Last time I saw one of those, it was wrapped around a duck's face. Left ducklings without a mother. You take that kill-bag with you and don't let me see it again!"

"I will and won't. I mean, yes, of course." Her squealing unnerved him. Luke was fully aware of the consequences of plastic pollution. Her harsh reaction reminded him once again of the pervasive problem. When she settled, he showed her a star stone.

Barbara nodded with an improved opinion of him. "Water plants, eh?"

She disappeared from view and reappeared from behind a clump of bog grass in a small canoe. Paddling it to a further corner of the pond, she instructed Luke, "Follow me."

He traversed water's edge and watched as Barbara used skilled strokes to steer her watercraft. Hardly disturbing the surface water with expert precision, she docked the canoe beside a log. Stepping out, she adjusted her waders, laid in prone position, reached into the water and pulled young pond lilies from their roots. Some were sprouting yellow flowers. She gathered and held them up. "This is what Willy wants and they won't stay alive for very long, so get them to him right away."

Luke reached down with his thumb and pointer finger to collect them. "Thank you." He handed her the star stone in exchange and watched her place it in the canoe.

"Nice canoe you have there," complimented Luke.

"This is a great canoe, sturdy as they come! It made the original journey to these parts, designed by my great-grandfather. The community helped build it and all pitched in to chop branches and carve the centerlines," pointing to the inside of the boat.

"They gathered strips of wood, softened and bent them into place." She pointed to the sides.

"A mix of sticky pine sap for bonding and waterproofing. And just look at this paddle. What a beauty," admiring it, she rubbed the smooth wood surface.

"Now, about that bell," Barbara said, calling out in the opposite direction. "Grinby! Oh, Grinby!"

A toad, about the size of a dime, appeared and sat at Barbara's feet. When she reached down to pick it up, it made a low murmur. It reminded Luke of the sound when gargling mouthwash. Sort of a low g-g-g-grumble.

Luke asked, "Whatcha got there?"

"His name is Grinby," she replied, her eyes fixed adoringly on the brown animal. He cuddled into her cradled arms and commanded her full attention, gazing into her round, attentive eyes. As she caressed his underside, the creature's arms and legs fell loosely, flopping in rhythm with Barbara's bounces. She spoke to him then, in what can only be described as a series of croaking noises punctuated by different volumes and unusual pitches.

Luke's eyes widened at the sight of Grinby nestled in Barbara's arms. The toad was smiling at her. Did toads smile? Was that even possible?

Barbara's gentle cooing was both curious and comforting. Luke watched and wondered what it might feel like to snuggle a toad.

Why wouldn't she have a frog? It seemed more appropriate for a bog. Gradually, he began to accept the strange sight before him. Swept away by the image of a sprite nuzzling a squishy, leathery amphibian, Luke realized his own mouth was wide open. He snapped it shut.

"Watch this," Barbara said. She placed Grinby on the ground and imitated the sound of the bell (quite accurately) and pointed to the area where Luke had dropped it.

"What did you say to him before?" Luke wondered.

"I told him I had a big slug and a fat bug if he found the bell, or something like that. He understood well enough."

They watched as Grinby hopped over clumps of bog grass and swam along the surface water.

"He swims pretty well for a toad," Luke said.

"Yes, I trained him and between us, I'm quite certain he thinks he's a frog," Barbara replied, all the while never taking eyes off her pet.

When Grinby dove at the spot where Luke dropped the bell, bubbles surfaced. Seconds later, Grinby popped up with bell in mouth and headed back to his mistress.

Luke was certain he saw the toad smile. Oh, yes, now the "grin" part of his name made sense.

Grinby dropped the bell at Barbara's feet.

"There you go," she said, picking it up and offering it to Luke, gleaming with pride at the success of her beloved pet. She motioned for Grinby to get in the canoe and paddled them away without another word.

Luke watched her depart in the direction of the beaver lodge. Sunlight reflecting off the water made it difficult to tell where she went, or did she disappear?

He placed the bog plants in the plastic bag. Though he understood the environmental damage caused by plastic, bags were handy when it came to transporting or storing things. Convenience often trumped environmental protection, unfortunately.

Returning to his car, he checked the time and though he wanted to stop at his apartment for a change of clothes, he knew he couldn't. He was muddy and damp, but he needed to get the plants to Willy.

CHAPTER 7

Bob waved to Luke. "Hey! Where ya been?"

"Lunch break."

"Looks like you took a dip in the river." Bob walked over to a nearby stack of t-shirts, found a medium and handed it to Luke. "Here, put this on. What's that?"

"This?" Luke lifted the bag with roots, green sprouts, yellow buds and droplets of water.

Bob grimaced, ever shocked with what some people ate in the name of organic or raw or vegetarian or whatever diet craze was popular. When Luke saw him shaking his head, he asked, "What's up?"

"The special order arrived. A video probe, wasn't it?" Together, they walked to the office.

Luke placed the plastic bag with bog plants behind his computer monitor and left to change his shirt.

Bob opened the box and unpacked its contents. He inspected the invoice, opened the directions and took a seat to read the accompanying information about how to use the slim, endoscopic camera attached to a flexible cord. "This is some piece of equipment, says here it captures high resolution audio and visual with illumination. Do we need audio?"

Luke had just returned and connected the probe to his computer. "Sure! We want to capture the whole experience!"

It took a minute for the computer to recognize a new device. He pointed the video probe around the room and watched the images on his monitor. "Yup, works like a charm," he announced to encourage Bob to stop reading the instruction manual. "I still need to test it on my phone, but that'll have to wait."

Bob took the hint, filed the invoice in one location and the instruction book in another, and showed Luke that if he needed it, it was, "right here."

Luke nodded. In the unlikely event that Luke ever needed to consult directions about the video camera probe, he would search online first.

"I'll leave you to it then," Bob said.

The moment Bob was gone and the door closed, Luke blurted, "It was amazing down there, Gretchen! She had a pet frog, no, a toad, named Grinby."

"That's weird," Gretchen remarked.

"Weird doesn't even begin to describe it," he said, grabbing his turkey wrap and iced tea from the fridge and a bag of chips from his desk drawer. "I'm starving."

Gretchen reported, "I found records about Charles. He worked here in 1973. The general manager was a guy named David." She waited and watched as Luke devoured his lunch. "Can I see the plants?"

Luke pointed and Gretchen walked over to them. "Oh look! They're so little and cute and green!"

"Little, cute, green?" Luke imitated, smiling at her enthusiasm. "Barbara said to take them to Willy right away, so I'll go..."

Luke stopped when Bob entered the office. "I thought you just had your lunch break."

"Growth spurt?" Luke resumed eating and chewing, but had some difficulty swallowing as Bob watched.

"Right," Bob replied, organizing papers at his desk and checking email while Luke ate. And that was all he said about that. Luke was an excellent worker and he wasn't going to make a big deal about it if Luke took time away from the park.

Bob looked up occasionally to monitor Luke's progress and after he saw him down the last sips of an iced tea, Bob proceeded. "I've got a few hours to spare, so I thought we could review the video together."

Luke motioned for Bob to pull a chair over as he repositioned his computer monitor for both to get a good view of the project. A sideway glance and nod from Luke was all Gretchen needed. It would be up to her to get the plants to Willy. She lifted the bag, careful to avoid Bob's notice.

"I'm going to lunch now!" Gretchen announced and mouthed the words to Luke, "I got this."

Luke was relieved to have her help and soon realized she would need additional guidance. Moments after she left the office, Luke grabbed a paper clip from his desk drawer and leaped to his feet. "Nature calls!"

Bob leaned back in his chair, confused about how a paper clip was necessary for a call from nature. But, he just replied, "I'll be here."

Luke ran outside and caught up with Gretchen. "You need a bell to get Willy's attention." He showed her the delicate, cylindrical bell and tried to open the paper clip, intending to feed it through the loop on top of the bell, fumbling. "I really have to stop chewing my fingernails." As he struggled, a family walked past.

"Here, let me do it," Gretchen easily attached the paper clip to the tiny cannon and shook it to listen for its ring. "I can barely hear it." She turned it upside down to look for the clapper and found only a thin rod. Without a ball at the end, it made only a slight sound. She rang it again.

Luke watched the children who walked past them turn around and look for the sound while their parents didn't seem to notice. Only the kids heard the bell. Interesting, he thought.

"Enter Bear's Den, ring the bell a few times and wait. If he doesn't come out, look for an opening after the second light on the right. Leave the plants there. Good luck."

"Right. If he doesn't show, I'll leave the plants."

In one hand she held the bog plants and in her other, the tiny, brass bell. The thought of meeting a magical creature made her nervous, but it also gave her a feeling of purpose and satisfaction to know she would be helping the little people.

Gretchen chatted with the guide at the caves entrance to quell suspicions. After their friendly banter, she said, "Great day to get some exercise," and headed up.

When she reached the cave, she entered, rang the bell and waited.

When hikers approached, she offered a weak excuse for her lengthy stay in the cave. She knew very little about geology, but recalled seeing a sign for pegmatite. "Wonderful sample of pegmatite here. Lovely crystals. Excellent specimen," she said as they squeezed around her.

Gretchen rang the bell again and waited.

She looked at the granite rocks above her and thought about the forces of nature that sent boulders crashing down to create the caves fifteen to twenty thousand years ago. Pink sparkles glimmered as sunlight bounced from one of the granite surfaces. The quiet and protection calmed her and as time passed, she grew more resolute in her decision to wait as long as necessary for Mr. Willy Topper to appear.

Luckily, the rush of visitors today had been earlier and no additional visitors approached. As she waited, a sound of movement came from the nearby opening. She held her breath in anticipation of who might show himself from the precipice before her.

No one appeared. Gretchen jumped when a squeaky voice emanated from the opening. "Do you have the plants?"

Startled by the unusual pitch of his voice. She blurted, "Yes!" and placed them at the opening.

"Thank you."

"Oh, but I wanted to meet you... to see you."

"Where's Luke?"

"He sent me."

"That was not our agreement." Willy snatched the bag of plants and pulled them into the hidden cave.

Gretchen watched the plants disappear and moved closer to the crevice. She whispered in the sweetest tone she could muster. "Luke couldn't come here to deliver the plants, but he wanted to get them to you as quickly as possible. Only Dean and I know about you, but that's because Luke trusts us and so can you. Please don't worry. You don't have to show yourself. I understand. It must be terribly frightening for you."

Willy leaped to the outer edge of the small cave entrance and announced, "I am not afraid!"

Gretchen peered at the wee man, eyes wide at the sight of an incredible miniature before her. The golden sparkle from his eyes especially caught her attention. "I'm Gretchen. It's so very nice to meet you, Willy!" She flashed a smile and lifted her hand to extend a handshake but quickly lowered it too, suddenly aware of how impossible it would be to shake hands with the tiny man.

"It is my pleasure to meet you." He bowed and removed his hat to formalize their introduction.

Gretchen giggled at his dramatic gesture and said in a soft voice, "Luke told me about your community. I only want to help and I'm so very curious. How did you ever get here?"

Willy considered her question. "Now, that would take some time to explain."

She flashed him another smile.

Willy scrutinized her. It was different talking to a female Mort. Her scent was like flowers that popped after a thaw. Her eyes were outlined with dark paint and he studied the shape and admired their beauty. Her lips looked orange-red, the color of leaves after the first freeze, and shiny, as though ice crystals had been sprinkled on them. The sound of her voice was a mixture of wind chime and birdsong.

Should he trust her? Willy's insides felt comfortable and calm, even a bit happy. All good signs. He admired the size and shape of her white teeth and said, "I'll be right back."

Gretchen's heart leaped with excitement. What good fortune! Willy Topper was here and he was coming right back! She would ask if she could record him. Luke would be so impressed if she captured his story.

Willy returned to the crevice opening a few minutes later holding a three-legged stool.

"What's that?" Gretchen asked.

"My chair." He lifted the stool sideways for her to appreciate the craftsmanship. "We braid soft twigs for the legs and criss-cross pine cone scales like so... and then we weave a pillow and stuff it with silky hairs from milkweed pod for the cushion, that is unless we can get the first feathers of ducks. We prefer the small feathers right after eggs are laid, but they're harder to come by."

He set the stool down and repositioned it until he was sure it didn't wobble. "I stubbed my foot a while back and well, let's just say, I'm doing my best to keep weight off it."

"Before you begin, I wanted to know, can I tape you?"

"With sticky stuff?"

"Oh, no, I meant record or capture your voice on my phone. That is, if you don't mind..." Gretchen was cautious about overstepping her opportunity. She paused and remained quiet, thrilled to be conversing with this endearing, small person, careful not to push or pester.

Willy understood what her request meant now, recalling how Luke captured his voice. He knew about the Google voice and the music from Luke's phone. Talking into the phone hadn't resulted in any negative consequence, however, the touching of a phone, well, that was another matter entirely.

He wondered, had phones replaced books?

In the past, Charles provided books. Books carried the Mort's words, their language and their life. Books had enriched his life, indeed, the lives of all Toppers, allowing them to discover the world of Morts with their different manners and customs. Storing words on the phones seemed to be the way of it now. Things had changed.

However words were shared, to Willy, telling a story about an ancestor was to greatly honor them. Recounting tales was a celebration of life in his society. Since he felt no fear in the telling or recording, as it was, he was inclined to agree to her request.

Gretchen watched as Willy deliberated. He was delightful, so absolutely appealing and dare she say, cute? He had a pudgy, affable appearance.

Finally, he said, "You may record our story, Gretchen."

She offered a wide smile. "Thank you! Watch this, Willy." She touched the recording button and held the screen up for Willy to see. Then, she nodded for him to begin.

Willy began. "Here's how we got to this spot. Well, look at that." He pointed to the blue line moving along the screen as it registered audio waves of his voice. Careful not to touch the device, he marveled at the science of it.

Gretchen smiled and encouraged him with wide eyes as if to say, yes, it's amazing that this device can record your story and you should continue.

He continued. "Our ancestors lived in Canada when ice covered most of the world. That is, until the great melt. Temperatures rose too quickly and my great-grandfather, Rufus, a well-respected and very wise leader, recognized the trouble. Waters were rising, their homes, threatened."

Gretchen interrupted him and stopped recording when she heard conversations of approaching park visitors. "Hang on, Willy, let's just wait for these hikers to pass." She blocked their view of Willy by leaning against the cave wall and allowing as much space as possible for the hikers. She also offered an explanation of why she must remain in the cave pertaining to her interest in rock formation.

The family of five shimmied and squeezed around Gretchen.

She wished them a good day and prompted Willy, "Okay, let's continue."

Willy resumed his storytelling. "They didn't want to leave their home. It was an ideal spot. Generations worked to create the place they called Grotte Sécurisée Connectée. French Morts call the place Montagnes Laurentiennes. You know it as the Laurentian Mountains. Translated, their home was Safe Connected Caves.

They had the best water, food and shelter. Anything needed or wanted was there: plentiful, soft moss, star stones, heated ponds, clean water, spacious rooms and passages leading one to another. Outside there was a small stream for water sports and fishing. They had pits to lure grouse and ancient piles of hobblebush to attract squirrels. There were rope swings, ladders and tree branches to climb for nuts and berries."

Willy stopped and raised his hand. Gretchen paused the recording and listened. She could hear distant warbling of birds, but nothing else. A second later, two young boys crouched to enter the cave and stopped when they saw Gretchen. She smiled and said, "Just checking on some of the rocks here," she chattered on about feldspar and quartz as they quickly passed her. When she turned around, Willy was gone. He had taken the stool and disappeared into the crevice.

"Nice one, Willy. I didn't hear them coming." Gretchen looked at the charge on her phone, 5%, and hoped it had enough power to capture all of his story. Willy reappeared, sat on his stool and continued.

"No one wanted to leave Safe Connected Caves, so Rufus had his work cut out. Though all the signs were there: rising waters, birds taking flight, intense heat from the sun, they were a stubborn bunch. But, Rufus was persistent.

The changes meant danger, he told them. Finally, the loss of birds and most notably, the absence of woodpeckers, convinced them of the threat. To us, the drumming of a woodpecker means good luck and no one had heard one for a very long time. That was it. They accepted their fate. If Elves wanted to survive, they needed to move."

Willy paused to adjust himself on his stool and Gretchen asked, "So, before you came here you were called Elves?"

"For many generations, Morts called us Elves, but that changed when we came here. We created new names for our new beginnings, our new homes."

"Toppers? Why Toppers?"

"Are we not on top?" Willy swept his arm in the direction of the valley below.

Gretchen agreed.

Willy resumed. "To depart, my ancestors needed to build sturdy canoes. It was an immense undertaking and one that had to be completed very quickly, as you might imagine.

The journey was fraught with peril. All manner of obstacles presented themselves: logs, boulders, ice chunks, whirlpools, harsh turns. At night they secured their boats to whatever was available, a tree or outcropping of rocks, and tried to sleep. Lost mittens, a scrape or bruise, all easily remedied, but then, tragedy struck.

On the fifth travel day, Rufus awoke from a nightmare with such a startle, he fell from his canoe into the frigid waters. He shrieked and lunged, as if fighting off an imaginary enemy. Weighted with furs and hide, he was carried away by the current, never breaking the surface water. Gone.

The survivors held a ceremony and said their goodbyes. He would be greatly missed. Without Rufus to guide them, his three children: Drew, Tucker, and Betty quibbled. Who should take over? When and where should they stop?

The eldest, Drew, took charge and two days after losing Rufus, he directed all canoes to stop at the place with outcroppings of rocks and markings on a cliff. This very cliff. He led a group of brave climbers into and through the caves. The arrangement was deemed satisfactory and Drew was convinced they must make it work for them.

Most followed Drew; he was my grandfather. Betty and her group left to make their home at the pond. Tucker led others who found comfort in the trees.

We're three clans now. Toppers live here, in the deep caves above the valley. Boggers live at the bog and are known as Waterfall Down Lodge. And, Loggers live in dry tree hollows of the forest and are Cranny Nook Circle."

Willy stood, placed his hands on his hips and removed his red cap, ran his fingers through his hair and gently patted his head, as one might do in a show of gratitude, as if to say, "Thank you, brain," before replacing his hat.

Gretchen stopped the recording and saw it had registered just under five minutes with 2% power remaining.

"Thank you, Willy! That was amazing."

"My pleasure!" he boomed. "You're a good listener. And now, I have a great favor to ask of you. Is it possible for you to get me a book? Do they still exist?"

"Yes, books still exist," Gretchen said with a chuckle. "A miniature one, I presume?"

"The smaller the better!"

"I will certainly try," promised Gretchen.

Tipping his hat while offering a dramatic bow, he said, "Good day to you, Miss Gretchen." Willy collected his stool and disappeared into the recesses of his cave dwelling.

Gretchen departed, bubbly with excitement. It would be hard to contain her eagerness, but she knew she must remain quiet to protect the Toppers. The history of how little people came to live in Rumney was on her smartphone! Luke would be so impressed.

As she had listened to Willy's story, she felt a kinship grow between them and when he complimented her for being a good listener, it lifted her spirits. She wondered how Willy had developed such refined manners. He was so very polite. His etiquette and courtesy seemed old-fashioned.

Had good manners become obsolete? Earlier that day at a coffee shop, a man in a hurry let a door close in front of her. She nearly walked into it. And she remembered at a slow checkout line last week, a person cut in front of her and others who had been waiting much longer. Willy had the right idea.

Extending common courtesies made everyone's life better.

Gretchen paused to gaze up at the rock face known as Hawk's Cliff. She considered it differently now. It was more than just a place to hike through granite boulders. It was Willy's home.

CHAPTER 8

Gretchen returned to the office and quickly charged her smartphone. She swayed to and fro, stretched her arms, squatted in deep knee bends and paced around the room. The pile of vegetables were still on her desk, but who could eat? Surely it had been difficult for Luke to keep Willy a secret, but she knew it was harder for her.

Bob acknowledged Gretchen. "How was lunch?"

She tilted her head thinking about how to respond. "Productive."

Bob furrowed his brows. "Productive? How's that?"

"Got some exercise."

"Looks like you're still getting it," Bob replied.

Luke didn't say a word. His warning glare said it all.

Gretchen forced herself to sit and relax.

Luke and Bob returned to viewing the film of ducks, swimming and dabbling. "I like the panoramic of the pond. Let's take off the first ten seconds and start it when the ducks are bobbing for weeds. Keep the group shot when they fluff their feathers." Bob suggested. "They look happy."

Gretchen dug through her purse to keep her hands busy. She organized items in the top drawers of her desk for no particular reason and checked her smartphone to see when the battery symbol changed from red to green. When Luke glanced over at her, she deliberately widened her eyes and nodded in the direction of the device, once, twice, thrice, like a bird popping from a cuckoo clock. When Bob turned to look, she froze.

Temptation to check the recording she captured was powerful. Too powerful. She just *had* to make sure it worked! As soon as her phone was charged enough to function, she activated the recording: *Here's how we got to this spot.* Yes!

Luke stopped. "What was that?"

Gretchen mouthed, "Oops."

Bob asked, "What was what?"

Relieved, yet alarmed, Luke said, "Why don't you pull a chair over here, Gretchen? You need to see some of the changes Bob and I made."

Together they noted minor modifications to the video of the park. Gretchen complimented Bob's suggestions. He had a knack of capturing the best flora and fauna since he knew it best. She would have to re-record two segments. As they wrapped it up, Bob suggested, "Let's have Dean take a look at this too. Nice work, both of you."

"Thanks, Bob." Luke stood to stretch his legs and give his eyes a rest. Film editing wasn't strenuous, but it certainly took a lot of concentration.

After Bob left, Gretchen headed back to her smartphone. "Listen to this." *Our ancestors lived in Canada when ice covered most of the world. That is, until the great melt.* She paused it. "Can you believe it? He let me record the story of how they got here!"

"Shhhh," Luke replied. Gretchen's enthusiasm was one of the best things about her, but she needed to keep it down. "Obviously you could hear him."

"Yes!"

"What happened with the plants?"

"At first he wanted me to leave them. He was upset that it was me and not you, but I explained. I put on the charm..." She winked and flashed Luke a mischievous smile. Luke returned it with a slight blush.

She continued. "Willy sent the plants down to be planted or whatever they do and came back, sat on a stool and told me the story. Don't you just wish you could see their community?"

"Yes, but we have to keep it on the low down. Agreed?"

"Agreed. Sorry. It's hard to contain the wonder of it all. But, I will. I promise. He asked me to get a book for him."

"He asked me that too." Luke turned in his chair to show Gretchen what he had already found on the Internet. "There's actually a Miniature Book Society and publishers who specialize in miniature books. Did he say what kind he wanted?"

"No, he didn't specify."

"What's your favorite book?"

"That's easy. Any of the Harry Potter books."

Searching on the web, they discovered a miniature book created by J.K. Rowling. It was auctioned off for charity a couple of years ago for $100,000. Seriously out of their price range.

"Pick something else," Luke suggested.

"What's available? Most of these titles I've never even heard of." They scrolled through books online. "How about a dictionary?" Gretchen suggested. They found one with two day shipping. Affordable. Done.

"Let's see what you found out about Charles," Luke said.

Gretchen pulled a folder from her desk drawer labeled Employees 1973. Charles Haarin, Address, Phone Number, Emergency Contacts, References. "These details are out-of-date. I called the phone number and they told me I had the wrong number, but at least we know his last name."

Luke put Charles Haarin into his computer's search engine and found a Facebook page. "A friend request won't work. He doesn't know me."

"But he knows Polar Caves," Gretchen suggested. "If he follows that Facebook page, we could contact him."

"Only Bob has access and we can't risk telling anyone else about Willy."

"Check it out," Gretchen lifted a lamp from Bob's desk to reveal sticky notes with his logins and passwords. "Try this: theboss and pass123."

"How did you know that?" Luke asked.

"I pay attention," she beamed.

Luke signed into the park's Facebook page and scrolled through names of followers. "There he is! Charles Haarin. That was lucky. Okay, now we need to send him a message without revealing too much, you know, play our cards close to the vest," Luke said.

Gretchen suggested, "How about, Remember Willy? It's simple, to the point, no location, no last name, no details.

"I like it," replied Luke. He typed: **Remember Willy?**

"Now, we wait." Luke took a deep breath and logged out of the social media site.

"I wish we knew more about Charles. If only there was a way to get more information about him," Gretchen said.

"Maybe an FBI probe?" suggested Luke.

"Very funny. Okay, now I'm hungry. Time for my crudités."

"What did you just say?"

"Crudités, it's a French word for raw vegetables and dip." Gretchen pulled a container of dip from the refrigerator and uncovered the pile of vegetables on her desk. Selecting a raw zucchini, she scooped ranch dressing and chomped. Luke watched her with amusement. She had just dipped a large radish when Dean arrived.

"Those are some healthy snacks you got there, Gretchen. Remind me of my uncle who ate radishes every day to control his blood pressure."

Under his breath to Luke he mumbled, "wicked bloated most 'a the time."

Then back to Gretchen, "Never developed a taste for 'em personally." Dean shook his head with mild repulsion. "No sir, can't say I ever liked radishes."

Gretchen finished chewing and whispered loud enough for Dean to hear. "I met Willy!"

Dean froze in his tracks. "You met Willy?" He looked over at Luke for an explanation.

Luke explained, "She delivered the bog plants. I was going to take them up when I got back, but Bob wanted to see the video. I couldn't very well put him off, especially since I'd already been gone for almost two hours."

Gretchen whispered again to Dean. "And I could hear him, too!"

"Well then, now, that's somethin' I've been thinkin' about it. I'll bet you dollars to donuts loud rock-n-roll wrecked my hearin'," Dean said matter-of-factly. He took a seat and sighed. "So, it's just the three of us who know about the Lilliputians."

Gretchen scrunched her eyes, perplexed at the word Lilliputian. "What's that? Spell it." Dean complied.

She typed L-i-l-l-i-p-u-t-i-a-n into Dictionary.com, and read, "An inhabitant of Lilliput, a very small person. Where is Lilliput?"

Dean explained. "Lilliput is an island from *Gulliver's Travels*. Lilliputians were just six inches tall."

Gretchen nodded with when she recalled the novel, "Oh right!"

Luke interjected. "Dean, I think you're onto something."

"About Lilliputians?"

"No, about hearing loss. Over time, people hear less. It has more to do with age than rock concerts, though I'm sure the concerts didn't do your ears any favors. But my point is that as people get older they lose the ability to hear higher frequencies. Gretchen and I have, um, I guess you could say we have young ears."

"The missus thinks I should get hearing aids, but I'm not interested. World's too noisy, if you ask me."

Luke smiled and asked, "Gretchen, what did you notice about Willy's voice?"

"How cute it was."

"Right, it's cute because it's a high pitch. If I can convert the pitch to make it lower, Dean might be able to hear Willy speak."

Dean added, "And a bit more volume wouldn't hurt."

Luke rummaged through his desk and found a flash drive. "Gretchen, I need you to make a copy of the recording." He inserted the thumb drive into a USB interface on her computer and explained the process to upload and copy the file. After he had a copy of it, he would run it through a voice conversion process.

"Right. So, Bob suggested I take a look at the video you've created," said Dean.

Luke readied the video for Dean on his computer and snuck over to Bob's for a quick check of the park's Facebook page. No response yet.

"I need some fresh air," Luke announced as he spied one last chunk of zucchini on Gretchen's desk. "Mind if I take this?" he asked.

She handed it to him, curious why he would want it. Without ranch dressing, it didn't taste like much.

The end of the work day approached. A few visitors lingered in the gift shop, but most had departed. Luke walked to the animal park and stood looked out over the pond.

The waterfowl gathered under the shelter of the trees as the sun fell in the horizon. He snapped the chunk of zucchini into bits and threw it. Ducks quickly swam over and snatched the pieces. Then, he picked up scattered pieces of corn kernels and thought about what Willy said about the danger of feeding them "white stuff."

Oh, the life of a duck here. To wait for the toss of a few kernels of corn.... He amused himself with the thought that Gretchen's diet, her crudités, as she called them, would be good for these ducklings. Maybe the gift shop should sell fresh vegie packs for ducks.

He appreciated the view of straight, tall pines and the path leading up to the mountain when a hawk caught his attention. He watched it circle and land. A moment later, the hawk was heading to the valley. Something was up, he thought, as he bolted for Bear's Den past other staffers who were leaving for the day. "Any visitors still up there?" he asked them.

"No, all clear," one replied.

Luke ran up the stairs and along the boardwalks. Standing just outside Bear's Den, he split his time looking up for approaching hawks and looking inside for Toppers. On one glance inside, he saw a light glow and approached.

"Willy? Is that you?"

The light glow remained stationary.

"Topper?"

He heard a stone drop and a small female creature appeared. "Hello. I'm Shirley," she said, with the familiar squeak of her ilk.

Luke crouched lower to introduce himself. Shirley, in turn, explained that she knew all about

95

him from Willy and thanked him for the new water flow system, which was working very well, indeed. As she spoke, Luke admired her heavy black cape adorned with glittering gems and a large attached hood decorated with fluffy goose down. Her boots resembled those he had seen on Willy only smaller, not as bulky. Luke was naturally curious about the hawk activity. "Is something wrong? Are you leaving the caves?"

"It's the Boggers. They need our help."

"What's happened?"

"A few of the children are sick. Willy and Buddy have gone to bring them here. I'm their last hope, but I don't know if I'll be able to help them either. Barbara has already given them elderberry and root of Echinacea, but she's seen no improvement."

"What are their symptoms?"

"Fits of tummy trouble, aches and grumbles, and according to Barbara, it has been going on for much too long."

"Any idea how they got sick?" asked Luke.

"They like to ride on beaver tails. It's a new sport the young have invented. They connect a harness, a series of ropes from the beaver's teeth to their tails. The kids stand on the tail and when they yank on the rope, the beaver gives them a most exciting ride. Fun, but dangerous. When they fall off, which they usually do, they gulp pond water and that is what, we believe, has made them sick."

"Is there anything I can do?"

"The truth of it is, Luke, I would very much appreciate any help you could offer. Losing a young one, well, it would be just terrible, most tragic. Our water purification is the best and Barbara thinks our water will be better for them. But, I don't know what more I can do. Elderberry and root of Echinacea have worked in the past." Shirley shook her head, thinking aloud, mumbling a list of other types of herbs and remedies, Luke guessed.

"I'll see what I can do," he offered and darted out of the cave and down the path.

Gretchen was packing to leave for the day when Luke returned. "Bogger kids are in trouble. Shirley needs our help."

"Okay, slow down. Who's Shirley?"

"She's a Topper. She's worried about two of the Bogger kids. Their illness might have something to do with contaminated water in the bog. She said they've been riding beaver tails for fun and ingesting water and she thinks it's what's making them sick."

"Riding on beaver tails? Wow. Not sure how that would even work, but okay, tell me their symptoms and I'll call my aunt; she's a nurse practitioner."

Gretchen described their symptoms to her aunt while Luke listened to Gretchen's side of their phone conversation.

"These kids, uh, well, they like swimming in the bog," Gretchen explained.

"Maybe drank some of the water. "Tummy troubles. You know..., yes, most likely.""

"They can't be seen. They uh, they're too shy."

"How do you spell that?" Gretchen asked, motioning for Luke to write it down as she spelled it. "G-i-a-r-d-i-a-s-i-s"

"The one pill option is definitely better for these, uh, kids."

"I know, I know. But, could I just get the sample from you anyway? Just one pill."

"You're the best!"

Gretchen terminated the call on her smartphone. "She thinks they have the g-word infection and she has antibiotics for them. I'll figure out the medication ratio and meet you here tomorrow morning with the dosage."

"What did she say when you said I know, I know?"

"She wanted to see them in her office and test for the infection. But, she's making an exception because, well, she's awesome!"

Gretchen jumped up from her chair and freestyle danced like a cheerleader. Luke watched her, unable to contain his laughter and for a moment, he thought he might like to dance around with her.

When she had expended her pent up energy, she handed Luke his flash drive. "This has Willy's story. See you tomorrow!"

Luke stowed the flash drive in his pocket and entered the g-word into his computer's search engine. He learned there was another term for it: beaver fever.

"Figures," he said.

He gathered his belongings and set out to get a replacement phone.

CHAPTER 9

The next morning, Gretchen was waiting when Luke arrived.

"My aunt gave me..." She held up a packet of powder and read the name slowly, pronouncing each syllable. "Ti-ni-da-zole. I crushed the pill. I also estimated the ratio of Topper child to human to be 1:75, which, quite frankly, is pointless because I don't have tools to measure such a miniscule dosage. Just tell Shirley to administer one pinch, with plenty of clean water."

"One Topper pinch. Got it."

"Here's the bell. I forgot I had it."

"Thanks, Gretchen." He wanted to hug her, but stopped himself. He gave her a smile instead, a token of his appreciation and less awkward.

Luke departed with the bell, the medicine and his new Samsung Galaxy S9 smartphone. He delivered the powder and asked Willy about sending a camera down to view his community. Willy suggested they wait a few days; their priority was caring for the Bogger children.

When he returned to the office, Gretchen was on the edge of her seat.

"Delivered," reported Luke.

"Now, we wait," she said, drumming her fingers on the top of her desk.

Luke powered up his computer and plugged earbuds into the audio port. "Listen to this, Gretchen," he said. Luke had converted Willy's voice to a lower pitch using an online conversion tool.

She listened. "It doesn't even sound like him anymore," she said, disappointed. "I like the original Willy better."

"That's the conversion. His frequency registered higher than a soprano. Now he's a baritone."

"Was it hard to do?"

"Easy peasy," Luke said with a tilt of his head and a smirk.

Gretchen wondered what it would be like to be as savvy with technology as he was. "Any update on Facebook?"

Luke checked. "Nothing yet. I almost hope we don't hear from him. Willy said he wanted to see him again, but I don't have the best feeling about it." Luke waited for her response. He wanted to know if she felt the same way.

"I agree. But, it's up to Willy. If and when Charles makes the trip here, it's because Willy wants him to visit."

Luke thought through scenarios of what could happen if the existence of Toppers was revealed. Newspapers, television stations, special interest groups, movie producers, all would want to know about the little people who lived in the caves. Scientists would clamber for a chance to study them. The notoriety would be harmful. Their way of life might be forever compromised or worse yet, destroyed. The park could never handle the demand or exposure. It would be chaos.

Growing increasingly uneasy, Luke fiddled with the video probe connection to his new smartphone and announced he was heading up to Lemon Squeeze to film. Exercise would help him settle thoughts of how he would protect Babbling Brook Society if and when the time ever came.

Gretchen followed his example and left for Serenity Shelter in pursuit of solace and inspiration. She breathed in the smell of the forest and listened to the peeps and chitters of birds. She watched marsh ferns sway in the wind and squirrels bound from tree to tree. A woodchuck scampered across lichen covered granite boulders. Relaxing with the natural world calmed her and helped her to write and think freely.

She stared across the lush greenery to one of the largest trees in the park, Old Man Maple. Gazing at it filled her with a sense of awe; an ancient tree like that made her feel small in comparison. She thought of Willy.

Gretchen let her imagination wander to his hidden underground cavern. She thought it might resemble a grotto, a cavern-like space with a waterfall and rays of natural light that glistened off crystal rocks.

She strolled over to Maple Lodge and purchased a favorite treat, maple cotton candy. Yum. Its sugary fibers melted away on her tongue. She finished it before returning to the office where Luke was busy at his computer and Dean had just stopped in for a visit.

Dean asked, "Did ya hear about the girl who fell in the duck pond today?"

Neither had, so he continued. "So, I'm loadin' the ATV with water for the deer and hummin' that song, the one we've been workin' on Luke. Man, has that ever turned into an earworm. Ya know, I've been practicin' it every chance I get and it's, well..." Dean tried to shake the song from his ears.

"You know the best way to get rid of an earworm?" asked Luke. He waited for either to respond.

Gretchen suggested, "I heard you can chew gum to get it out of your head."

"Just play the darn thing?" wondered Dean.

Luke offered, "I was going to recommend listening to something else entirely."

Dean continued. "Anyhow, I'm just mindin' my own business when I see this family by the pond throwin' bread to the ducks."

Luke interrupted. "What? They were throwing bread?"

"Ayuh."

"Don't let anyone do that again, Dean. Promise me, if you see anyone do it, just stop them. Okay?"

"Sure thing, but why?"

"It's bad for the ducks. They get sick, lazy; it's unhealthy."

"Makes sense," Gretchen added. "It's not their natural diet."

Dean was surprised and a bit confused by Luke's interest in protecting ducks. Rather than return to the duck issue, he returned to his story. "So, this family is over by the duck pond and the two kids, maybe twelve, thirteen years old, a girl and a boy, start arguin' about who gets to hold the bag of bread and the next thing you know the girl's soakin' in the pond!"

Luke asked, "How? There's a fence around it."

"She squeezed through to get closer to the ducks or to get away from her brother, who knows? He shoved her in and naturally, I headed over straight away to help. She was a mess, poor thing." Dean mimicked the girl shaking water from her hair and clothes, picking pond muck from her arms and legs.

"Then the ducks started goin' crazy, flappin' and quackin'. Oooee! Those ducks were mad about loosin' the bread or havin' a visitor, but the geese were the worst! Couple of those Canadian Geese were honkin' and hissin'. Ever heard a goose hiss?"

Neither had, so Dean mimicked the sound by pushing air from his tightened throat and extending his neck. Both agreed it sounded threatening and nasty.

"By the way, Luke, I pulled the bag of wet bread out of the pond, you'll be pleased to know, and tossed it in the garbage."

Luke was visibly appreciative. "Good," he said.

"I suggested they come back another day to hike the park. No charge. Gave 'em free passes for their next visit. Luckily no one was hurt but I gotta tell ya, it was quite the spectacle."

"Sibling rivalry, huh?" offered Gretchen, amused.

"More like pandemonium with the waterfowl gettin' so agitated," said Dean.

Gretchen recounted the health situation Luke chanced upon by way of Shirley telling him about the Bogger children and how her aunt was a medical professional and she procured medicine from her, but who knows if it would work?

"Whoa, take a breath, Gretchen!" Dean cautioned.

Luke added, "And on top of that, I'm still worried about how to keep the cistern water from freezing in the winter."

"Let me think about that one, Luke. I'm not sure solar is the best answer, but we'll figure somethin' out. You gotta take it easy, my man," Dean offered.

Dean could see both Gretchen and Luke were anxious. "Those pixies are stressin' you! It's time to call it a day. Are you two still headin' over to Meadowbrook?"

"You know it!" Gretchen pumped her arms, jumped up and down a few times, and prepared to leave.

Luke confirmed, "I'll pick you up at 6:00?"

"Sounds good." Gretchen bolted out the door.

Luke left the office and headed to Maple Lodge to troubleshoot a wireless router before he left for the day. It probably just needed a reset. On his way to the parking lot, his phone alerted him.

Gretchen texted: **r u still at park?**
Luke responded: **yes**
Gretchen: **lft my jacket can you bring it?**
Luke: **np**

He returned to the office and saw her jacket hanging on the back of a chair when he heard a thunk. Something hit the floor. He stopped and looked in the direction of the sound.

Dropping to his knees, he peered under the furniture and saw a cup had fallen to the floor. Someone or something had pushed it off. Reaching for it, he recognized it as the mug Bob used to hold rubber bands.

He picked them off the carpeting, refilled the cup and returned it to the desktop. That was strange, he thought, again looking around and under the furniture for the culprit.

He waited for more movement, listening and looking. A window beside Bob's desk was opened slightly, a couple of inches. That wasn't unusual, but he thought it best to close and lock it. So peculiar was this incident, he would have waited longer if he didn't have someplace to go. Gretchen, dinner and an outdoor concert were waiting. He picked up Gretchen's jean jacket, looked around one last time and left.

Bob was closing up, balancing the cash registers.

Luke stopped beside him. "I shut a window in the office, the one by your desk."

"Why? Did something happen?"

"I heard a noise and your mug of rubber bands was on the floor, so I picked it up. Any signs of mice?"

"No, but I've seen squirrels outside that window," Bob confirmed.

"Well, they're either locked in or out. I closed the window."

"I'll give it a look see when I finish here. Have fun tonight in Gilford."

"Thanks," Luke said, heading out of the lodge. On his way, he crossed paths with Danny, a fellow employee who he always stopped to chat with.

They talked about the venue in Gilford. Parking was easy; there were large viewing monitors and lots of options for food and drink.

Danny told Luke about the time he took a date to the place. He recalled, "She was a strange one... wild, crazy dancing and wouldn't you know, she ended up on the huge video screen for at least a minute. People around us were pointing at her and the screen. It was so funny. Then, like ten minutes later, a former boyfriend came around and said he spotted her up on the big screen and starts talking to her, and I'm just standing there. It was *so* awkward. She ended up sneaking away and leaving with him!"

Luke joked with him, bantering, "Oh, man, that's awful! Did you ever go out on another date with her?"

"No!" laughed Danny. "I'm sure you'll have a better time with Gretchen. She seems really nice."

"Yeah, thanks, man," Luke said. "Catch you later."

Walking the path to the parking lot, he checked the time and realized he should let Gretchen know he was running a bit late.

Luke texted: **omw**

He took a few more steps and abruptly haulted when something hit him on the side of his head. "Ow!" he yelled and looked on the ground for the projectile. It was an acorn.

He rubbed his head to ease the sting and looked around to locate the source. Was Dean playing a joke on him? Dean's truck was still in the parking lot, but he quickly reconsidered. That was *not* something Dean would ever do.

Another nut sailed past, missing him by a few inches. Whoever was hurling acorns had good aim. He ran to his car and grabbed binoculars. Peering through them, he scanned the forest.

He saw the usual: trees, leaves, birds, squirrels. Lowering his binoculars, he waited, searched again and heard high pitched laughter. It sounded like giggling or taunting.

When he again peered into the trees, following the sound, he saw squirrels running and jumping from branches. Were those light glows on their backs?

CHAPTER 10

Gretchen was waiting on her front porch step when Luke arrived. She hopped in his car and wondered, "Why so late?"

"Yeah, about that..." Luke continued after he merged onto 93 south. "So, I went back for your jacket and heard a thud. I looked around and saw Bob's mug, the one he uses for rubber bands. Someone or something had pushed it over. That's weird, I thought. Who or what knocked it off his desk? Never found out. Then, I stopped to talk to Danny and I'm walking to my car when an acorn comes sailing through the air and hits me right here." He touched the right side of his head.

"Are you okay?" Gretchen was bothered.

"Yeah, it's just a bump."

"Did you apply ice?" she asked.

"No."

"Let me see."

"It's fine.

"Come on!" She reached over to examine it. "You definitely have an egg. Is your vision okay?"

"I hope so. I'm driving," reminded Luke. He thought about his sighting of light glows on the squirrels' backs, but decided to keep that to himself. It seemed too mysterious. Instead, he asked, "How do you think Toppers transform into light glows? Ya know, when they squeeze a star-stone?"

"Magic," she answered. "It's like a Metamorphmagi from *Harry Potter and the Deathly Hallows.*"

"No idea what a Megamorphmagi is," replied Luke.

"They're wizards who can change their appearance. But now that I think of it, transforming to pure energy sounds more like an obscurus, you know, like in *Fantastic Beasts.* You saw that movie, didn't you?"

"No, I didn't catch that one," confessed Luke.

Gretchen gave him a look of disappointment and reconsidered her explanation. As she was an all things Harry Potter aficionado, she reassessed her initial assumption.

"Actually, an obscurus is made of dark energy so that wouldn't work in this situation. The little people change into energy, but it's not the evil kind. It's good energy and I believe, it's entirely unique."

"It definitely involves energy," agreed Luke. "If you consider the interchange of energy and mass in Einstein's..."

Gretchen interrupted him. "Can we just agree on magic? I *much* prefer it."

As they drove, each pondered their own ideas about how little people existed and how their mysteries might be explained. Gretchen thought about magic wands and potions. Luke thought about $E = mc^2$ and the science behind mass-energy equivalence.

Gretchen was first to break their silence. "I wish we could get a miniature Harry Potter book for Willy. He would love Harry, the quintessential hero." She waited for Luke's reaction.

"You like using big words, don't you?"

"Perhaps," she continued. "I'm sure Willy's community considers him their hero, or as you said, one who watches for the signs. And, you're a hero too, helping them with their ice shortage, getting the bog plants."

"I'm not sure about that. Dean, you, me... we've all helped out. You got the medicine," he returned.

"I hope it worked." Gretchen stared out the car window, introspective, wondering. What if the medicine did more harm than good?

Traveling to the concert, they drove along Lake Winnipesaukee. The lake was placid; boats sailed or motored along the open expanse of aqua blue set before the wooded shore. Mountains stood out in the distance and clouds dotted the sky.

They challenged each other to spell Winnipesaukee and wondered what it meant when translated. "Dean would know its translation and how to spell it." Luke suggested.

Gretchen was about to google its translated meaning, but stopped when she heard the sound of Luke's directional. They had arrived at the outdoor amphitheater.

There were enticing food choices and the concert was excellent, as expected. Jason's music floated through the pavilion and when *I'm Yours* played, Luke reached for Gretchen's hand.

On the drive home Gretchen asked, "Can we stop for ice cream? I'm craving real maple walnut."

"Sounds good. I could go for chocolate."

"With nuts?"

"I've had enough for one day." Luke jested.

"Ice cream makes everything better." Gretchen stated matter-of-factly and she was right. The ice cream was delicious.

Gretchen reminisced. "Whenever I eat it, I think of the times when I'd go out with my family. My sisters and I would chant *I scream; you scream; we all scream for ice cream* from the back seat of our minivan. Just the taste of it on a warm summer night takes me right back to those days."

After their frozen dessert, the drive back was a quiet one. Both were tired and neither felt the need for conversation.

Luke parked in front of Gretchen's home and asked her to wait until he walked around and opened the passenger door. Then, he escorted her to the front door and waited to be sure she was safely inside before leaving.

Saturday and Sunday were busy at the park. So busy, in fact, Bob reassigned Luke and Gretchen to work in Main Lodge. Monday and Tuesday were scheduled days off, but on Wednesday, they were back in the office putting finishing touches on the video.

"I'm going up to Bear's Den after work today and checking in with Willy. Hopefully I can send the probe down tonight."

"I'll meet you up there. The dictionary we ordered arrived and I want to give it to him. Look how cute it is!" She held up the book, two by two inches and about an inch thick. The writing was miniscule. "I had to use a magnifying glass to read it, but when I did, I could see it was the real deal. I know Willy has excellent hearing and now I'm thinking he must have amazing vision too."

Luke was at Bear's Den when Gretchen arrived. He rang the bell which he now wore hanging around his neck.

"Hello to you both!" Willy was in fine spirits when he appeared.

"How are the Bogger children?" Gretchen asked.

"Much improved! We sent them back to the bog. Barbara and Shirley extend their sincere thanks. Suffice to say, the children will not be riding beaver backs again."

"Did the medicine work?" Gretchen was eager to know.

"It did! We have always been of the mind that when an illness presents itself, a cure is close by. In this case, you were the cure." He bowed to Gretchen to show his gratitude and admiration.

"Oh, that *is* good news." Gretchen held out the red book with black lettering in her palm. "I have a book for you."

Willy retrieved it and read the cover aloud. "Dictionary."

He opened to a random page and picked a word. "Mirth - a noun - amusement, especially as expressed in laughter. There are many new words to learn, I see. Excellent, Gretchen. Thank you! This will be greatly appreciated by the entire Topper population."

"You're very welcome," she replied, feeling a delighted warmth spread through her.

Luke paused before asking, "Willy, would it be okay for me to send a camera probe into your community tonight? I have the technology with me."

"Yes Luke! We Toppers have always been a friendly bunch and you two are more than deserving of our hospitality. Send it down and I'll give you a tour. Shirley was putting acorn muffins in the oven when I heard the bell. If they're baked before your visit concludes, perhaps you'd even like to taste one. How's that sound?"

"Excellent! Let's go Gretchen." They departed the cave and Luke climbed up the rocks, positioning himself beside the cistern. He set the extension cable and the video probe by the same opening where the cistern's water tube disappeared into the crevice.

"Luke!" Gretchen called from the platform below, pointing about twenty feet away. "Can you see?"

A gray squirrel was shaking, thrashing its tail and stomping its feet as if having a seizure of some sort. It made a clicking sound.

Luke stared at the creature's antics and scanned other directions for signs of other nervous wildlife. "There's a couple over there too." He pointed across the granite boulders in the opposite direction.

Two gray squirrels glared, their postures erect, as if ready to attack. They screamed, "eey-yah, eey-yah!"

Gretchen yelled, "Luke! The cord!"

Luke whirled around to see the clicking squirrel scurry away with his extension cable. "Hey! Bring that back!" Luke demanded. But the squirrel was already beyond his reach.

"Can you believe it?" Gretchen sighed with exasperation.

Luke scowled at the other two squirrels who chatter-giggled and scampered away. Luke climbed down from the boulders, passed the equipment to

Gretchen and stood beside her, shaking his head in disbelief.

They returned to the cave and Luke rang the bell.

When Willy appeared, they told him what happened and waited for his response. It came after a few minutes of consideration, as was his way. After his deliberation, Willy explained, "The Loggers are behind this. They don't like Morts."

"What?" Luke blurted instinctively at the very instant his mind was connecting the acorn incident and squirrels hopping through the forest.

"Why such animosity?" Gretchen asked.

"Animosity? Might need to read that dictionary you gave me," Willy replied with a wink in Gretchen's direction.

Gretchen rephrased, "Why don't they like us?"

"It's complicated, but the main reason is this: their best tree hollow was cut down by a Mort. The curious thing is that it happened some time ago."

He shook his head and pulled his beard. He rubbed his hands together, lifted his hat, rubbed his hair, repositioned it again and said, "This calls for a meeting with Boggers and Loggers. I'll request it. Good evening to you both." He removed his cap, bowed and scooted away.

Luke and Gretchen left, disappointed. Their hopes of exploring a hidden community, dashed. Gone. Just like the cord Luke had special ordered.

Gretchen wondered, "Was it expensive?"

"About twenty bucks."

"Where would a squirrel even take it? I wonder if Dean might be able to help us get it back."

Luke agreed it was worth asking him. As they turned in the direction of Dean's workshop. Gretchen reached for Luke's hand. And why not? It was after hours. Her reassurance was comforting and he squeezed back with appreciation.

Dean saw them approaching. "Howdy do!"

Luke explained what happened to the extension cable and Gretchen interjected with details of the commotion from her perspective.

As Dean listened, he started to snicker.

Luke finished with, "... and the crazy squirrel skittered away with my cord!"

Now, Dean was outright laughing in his good-natured way. This started a chain reaction. Luke's anger began to dissipate and Gretchen couldn't help but smile at Dean's amusement.

Dean muttered, "I knew they stole nuts, but extension cables? That's a new one!"

Gretchen snorted, sending them all into fits. Their chortling and outbursts escalated.

When they calmed, Dean suggested they share a pop. He opened his cooler and grabbed three Moxies. "Got these up at a Moxie festival in July. That was some crazy time!"

Gretchen accepted the can and warned him. "Don't even get us started again! I don't want this coming out my nose." She sipped it. "It's sweet and bitter. Interesting."

Dean studied the can in his hand. "They make this stuff in the granite state. Bedford, I think it is. Good for your nerves." He downed the beverage and sat in his favorite chair, inviting Luke and Gretchen to pull up folding chairs and sit for a while. "My, my, my," he exhaled.

Luke chugged from his can and belched, trying to quell the sudden burst at the last instant, albeit unsuccessfully. "Oh, sorry."

They laughed again.

Dean looked out over the park and reflected. "Here's what I know. Those squirrels are clever, but they're not as clever as I am. I'm pretty sure I can find the cord. I know a few tree hollows I could check."

Gretchen considered the can she held. "Moxie means courage. So, if you drink this stuff, does it give you courage?"

"Indeed it does," replied Dean.

"Then, let's go get Luke's cord back!" She popped up and reached for Luke's hand, pulling him from his chair. Dean stood, ready to go.

Dean led them to an area near Serenity Shelter and pointed into tall white pines. "It's hard to see from here, but if you stand back just a bit, you can see a good sized tree hollow in that one, about forty feet up."

They studied it, looking up until Dean suggested, "Tell you what, you two go on along and I'll wait here a while and watch for any signs of the cable. If it's in there, I'll get it."

"How?" Luke wondered.

"I'm not inclined to divulge, but I'm resourceful, rest assured. You two, go on along. We've shared enough mirth for one day."

"Did you just say mirth?" Gretchen asked, unnerved by the coincidence of hearing that word again.

"Yes, I did. It's merriment, lightheartedness."

"I know what it means, I just..." She looked to Luke.

Luke explained, "Gretchen gave Willy a dictionary today. He opened to a random page and picked a word and it just so happened to be mirth."

"Serendipity! And, yes, I *do* believe in the cosmic forces that create it." Dean positioned himself against a nearby tree with an unobstructed view of the hollow. "See you both tomorrow."

As Luke and Gretchen made tracks away, they heard the tapping of a woodpecker. Dean announced, "Ah, yes, the fortunate yaffle of a tree-jobber."

Gretchen looked to Luke with a confused expression.

Luke explained, "He's referring to the woodpecker."

CHAPTER 11

The next day, Bob met up with Luke at guide's platform. Luke had just completed his morning hike through the caves and they descended together, pausing near the covered bridge. After discussing stories in the news, Bob sensed that something was bothering Luke; he seemed miffed. "What's up?" Bob asked.

Luke wouldn't tell Bob about his missing extension cable, but he would share something else that was irritating him. "Almost every morning I pick up empty water bottles left by hikers. We should do more to discourage the use of plastic here. What if we installed a purified water station and promoted it with reusable bottles?"

Bob said, "I'm listening."

"Some people think plastic bottled water is better for you, but the truth is, it's not always. A lot of bottled water is unregulated and all that plastic is bad for the environment. When you consider the cost to produce and transport it, that's a lot of fuel consumption. And then there's the recycling or landfilling aspects. I don't think we should sell plastic water bottles here at all. We should make it easy for visitors to fill bottles whether they bring them or if they purchase one at the lodge."

"That's a good idea," confirmed Bob.

Luke continued. "We have water stations at college that display the number of plastic water bottles saved from waste so you actually feel good when you refill your own container. Everyone needs to hydrate; it's just a matter of being more environmentally responsible. And, don't even get me started on plastic bags..."

"Tell ya what, I'll present the water station idea to the board at our next meeting. As for the bags, we could offer paper instead of plastic."

Luke felt better as they walked around the pond. "Hey, when did the loons arrive?" He pointed to two black and white water birds swimming side by side.

"Last night, I heard them calling out; it was eerie, sort of like yodeling."

They watched the loons dive and resurface. When guests stopped close by to also admire them, the loons stretched their necks, a stance they held when alerted to potential danger. The visitors stood motionless until the loons resumed their feeding.

"Glad they flew in for a visit," said Bob. "Not enough fish in there to keep 'em around for too long."

"Might catch a frog though," suggested Luke.

Then, moving on to the business at hand, Bob informed, "Dean's ready to install the high definition monitors today. So, did you catch the announcement in the paper about Saturday?"

"No, but if you posted it on social media..." Luke couldn't help himself. It was amusing to poke his boss when it came to their diverse habits using technology. "Dean mentioned that the park is hosting a free admission day for local residents."

"Right then. We're extending goodwill and promoting community spirit, giving the locals a chance to visit and see the improvements we've made. If the weather cooperates, it should be a good turn out."

"I like it." Luke patted Bob's back. "And, Gretchen told me the park will celebrate its 100th year soon. It'll be here before you know it."

"Maybe you'll come back and visit us in 2022? 'Course you'll be off making a six digit salary in Silicon Valley at some computer company."

"Maybe not Silicon Valley, but I do like the sound of a six digit salary." Luke laughed and continued on his way.

Gretchen greeted Luke as he entered the office and Dean came in shortly after, dangling the extension cord. "Look what I found," he said.

Luke hollered. "Yes!" Fist bump, "You rock!"

After their ceremonious affirmation of mutual admiration, Gretchen clapped her hands in praise of Dean's resourcefulness.

Luke plugged the cord into the video probe and tested. It worked. He followed with, "Okay, let's hear all about it."

Dean pulled over a chair and began. "After you left, I waited. Just sat there is all, watchin' the tree hollow and waitin'. A gray squirrel finally peaked out and gave a kuk."

"A kuk?" asked Luke.

"Kuks are what you call the clicking noises they make. Another squirrel stands alongside his kukking buddy; and he starts grunting, sounded like a pig, if you ask me. Then another squirrel caught my attention 'cause he was groanin'. I'm thinkin', by gosh if it doesn't sound like a barnyard out here! So the groaner squirrel comes runnin' across the ground and scampers up the tree, and what's he draggin'?"

Gretchen and Luke answered simultaneously. "The cord!"

"You got it. And who pops his little head out to receive the stolen item? None other than a tree elf! He was dressed in beige and brown and 'course I almost didn't see him, he blended in so well with the surroundings."

Gretchen blurted, "Camouflage."

"You better believe it," Dean confirmed. "But, I saw him and when he knew I saw him, you'll never guess what he did!"

Luke chimed in, "Threw a nut at you?"

"How'dya know?"

"I've been hit," touching the bump on his head.

"They're called Loggers and they hate us," said Gretchen.

"Why in heaven's name do they hate us?"

"We chop down their homes," said Gretchen, her eyes downcast.

Dean said, "So, let me get this right, Loggers don't like us because we chop down the trees they live in?"

Gretchen said, "That's what Willy told us."

"You *do* get the irony here, right?" Dean paused before he explained. "They call themselves Loggers but they don't like loggers."

"Well, yes, when you put it that way," Gretchen thought a moment and added, "Let's refer to tree cutters as lumberjacks to avoid confusion."

Luke was eager to hear more. "How did you get the extension cord?"

"Well, now, I'm gettin' to that. I cussed at the nut thrower and let him know I didn't appreciate gettin' hit, no sir, not one bit. Won't say here what I called the imp." He nodded respectfully at Gretchen. "So I grabbed my climbin' gear from the truck before settin' aloft."

"You climbed the tree?" Gretchen was most surprised to hear this.

"It was my dad, taught me to climb. He had a tree service. Supplied wood, mostly rock maple and rosewood, to Kelly Manufacturing. Back in the day, Rumney was famous for its crutches."

Gretchen clarified. "You mean like crutches for a broken leg?"

"Yes'm those exactly. Had a slew of government contracts over the years, but it's gone now, the building that is. Used to be over there on Stinson Brook, on the way to Rumney Rocks, if you've ever been out there."

"That's the rock climbing spot. I've been wanting to get over there," said Gretchen. "Have you climbed there?"

"I gave it a go a couple o' times. But, here's the thing about rock climbin'. It's not *if* you fall, it's a matter of *when*. I prefer trees. Much safer. Better traction. There's actually a path up the rocks that climbers call crutch factory and I wanted to try that on account of Dad's work, but it was, well, let's just say, it was out of my league. Not enough heel hooks or jugs, if you will."

Now Luke was curious, "You have climbing gear?"

"That would be my PPE." Dean waited for Luke's response.

"Not familiar with it," he admitted.

"It stands for Personal Protective Equipment, and yes, I have all sorts of gizmos. Ascenders, lanyards, carabiners, a harness, all the goods." Dean waved them in to move closer.

When they approached earshot, he whispered, "Wouldn't want Bob to know I was climbin' that tree. Are ya with me?"

Gretchen and Luke smiled at each other and nodded to Dean with unspoken agreement.

Dean continued. "I started the climb and as soon as Mr. Logger and the squirrels saw me headin' up, they skedaddled. The little guy disappeared altogether; never saw how he got away, and the squirrels scurried from branch to branch. Cowards! When I reached the hollow, I felt around and grabbed everything I could get my hands on."

He unzipped his backpack to show them. "This here's what ya call a trebuchet. It's different from a catapult 'cause it's got this counterweight, like so. And those Loggers have been borrowing office supplies," he said, snapping rubber bands attached to a slingshot made of a Y shaped branch. "Yessir, after I saw the elastics from the office, I took everything."

Luke said, "Rubber bands. Interesting...," as he and Gretchen inspected the weapons.

The slingshot was only an inch and a half tall. Side pieces of rubber attached a woven pouch to the ends of wood with tightly wound loops of rubber.

The slingshot was crafty, but the sophistication of the trebuchet was truly amazing. About twice the size of a Logger, it had a stand, a swing arm and a fulcrum, all made from a very strong wood, probably ironwood, guessed Luke.

Bolts carved from granite held the parts together. The counterweight was a jagged rock and was connected to the swing arm by woven rope. The pouch that held the payload was just the right size for an acorn, Luke estimated.

After thorough inspection of the goods, Gretchen suggested Dean should listen to the recording of Willy. She handed him her earphones and invited him to sit at her desk while Luke inserted the flash drive into her computer.

Luke explained, "I found an online tool called a pitch shifter. I lowered his voice by ten semitones and now he sounds mellow instead of squeaky." After the recording started, Dean increased the volume and gave a thumbs up.

As Dean listened, Luke borrowed seedless grapes from Gretchen to see if he could work the trebuchet. It was tricky, but after a few unsuccessful attempts, grapes were flying across the room and splattering.

Dean watched with amusement and Gretchen voiced her displeasure, saying she much preferred eating the grapes. Luke wiped grape juice from the wall, discarded the smooshed fruit and stowed the miniature weaponry in his desk drawer.

When Dean finished listening, he stood and stretched. "So, there's the three clans. Willy in the nether regions of the caves, Barbara with her beaver buddies and the Loggers who, as I can attest, seem a bit looney. Of the three, Toppers have the safest homes and to me, it's a shame they all don't live in the caves. I think that's why Willy is happier. He's safe and secure."

"And smarter too," Gretchen added. "He likes to read."

"When you're not worried about survival, you have more time for learnin' and story tellin'. It definitely sheds light on the pixies."

Dean looked into the distance, thinking. Gretchen and Luke expected his thoughts and waited.

He said, "Ya know, it is nothin' short of incredible that we have these elves livin' in and around the park. I always suspected there was mysterious happenin's around here, just never could put my finger on it, and now, knowin' this..." He stood a while longer and continued in a hushed tone. "We three, we're all gonna keep 'em a secret. Right?"

Gretchen and Luke agreed. Dean took in a deep breath and sighed. "I best get to work installing the monitors."

After Dean left, Gretchen burnt DVD's of their video while Luke wrote computer code. There was always computer work he could do to improve the efficiency of the business, linking point of sale with inventory, gathering visitor demographics to advertising efforts. Computers exceeded the speed and accuracy of human efforts in these areas and he put them to work.

Luke's thoughts returned to Willy. There had to be a way for Willy to use electronic devices without damaging them. To control electrical output, he would need a resistor of some sort, but it had work safely. He didn't want to hurt the little guy.

He remembered his middle school technology class with Mr. Martin, one of his favorite teachers. Luke thought back to the lesson when he volunteered to create static electricity. He shuffled across a carpet and discharged an electrical shock. After a class discussion of how and why the shock occurred, they learned about current. It was like water flowing through a pipe. Current was the flow and resistors controlled the flow. Pretty simple, really.

Mr. Martin asked, "What is current?" Luke's hand went up, as usual. He liked science and always paid close attention. But Mr. Martin had no intention of calling on anyone other than one girl whose eyes were glued to a page of doodling, her pencil busy creating lines and shapes. She answered his question with another (rarely a good idea). "Do you mean current, like events happening in the news, as in the present?"

The look on Mr. Martin's face was comical, but no one laughed. He shook his head in disbelief. Mr. Martin's solution to the situation was a pop quiz. At the end of class, he reviewed the girl's answers and scribbled a detention slip for her in return.

Luke saw the doodling girl later that day. He offered, "Bummer about detention."

She gave a weak smile and nodded.

He noticed she was wearing an unusual glove and asked about the black covering that protected only three of her fingers.

She was soft-spoken and explained that she liked drawing with pencils and chalk which meant a lot of smudging, so she made the glove to keep her hand clean. It covered her pinky, ring finger and palm, leaving her thumb, index and middle fingers free. Only the part of her hand that hit the paper was covered. Clever, he thought.

And that was it. Gloves! Willy needed gloves. Capacitive screens didn't work if you were wearing gloves because cloth prevented electrical current from passing. Willy needed gloves that had just the right amount of metal in them, conductive thread, to limit his electrical charge. Yes!

"Gretchen!" Luke called out. "I think I have a solution to control Willy's electrical current."

She was pleased he interrupted her for a change. He described the lesson from middle school, the girl and her gloves.

When he finished, Gretchen said, "Really? You were like Hermione Granger in Professor Snape's class. Did you ever see the deleted scene from Sorcerer's Stone, you know, when Snape puts Harry on the spot?"

Luke hadn't seen the movie or any deleted scenes either.

My point is that Hermione knew all the answers and she was a know-it-all, just... like... you." She pointed each word into his chest with her finger. Luke was charmed.

Gretchen powered down her computer, handed Luke the finished DVD's and reported, "I've got to run errands and Bob gave me the afternoon off. But, I'll be back after hours to help you send the probe down to BBS."

"BBS?"

"Babbling Brook Society" she said, whispering in his ear. "We need to keep it on the low down."

"Oh, right," he agreed. "Hey, could you leave me the rest of your grapes?"

CHAPTER 12

L uke waited for Gretchen at Bear's Den, wondering what errands she'd run that afternoon. As he waited, he listened for birdsong. Most calls he recognized, but a different one caught his attention. It had high chips, rapid trilling and when it finally flew, Luke saw its yellow underside and yellow at the end of its tail, as if a brush was dipped in paint. It joined another of its kind to gather blackberries from a bush.

He opened the Audubon app on his phone. Scrolling through the possible matches, he discovered it was a Cedar Waxwing and matched its chirps to the sound on the website which described its call as a "thin lisp, tsee."

Holding his phone in the air, he activated the call and watched the real birds react to the sounds of recorded bird calls. Their reaction amused him. He logged his sighting.

Waiting in the shade, the sun fell closer to the horizon and Luke considered the feasibility of using solar power for the cistern. The solar panel would need to be pointing south at a 70 degree angle in winter (given the latitude of Rumney). That would be tough, he reasoned. Wind power would be a much better option, but hiding a turbine wouldn't be easy. Though it would pale in comparison to the Tenney Mountain windmills, it would need to be large enough to catch wind...

His thoughts were interrupted by the view of a floating hawk heading in his direction. He shied away and ran from Bear's Den, fled to the far end of Raven's Roost, descended the stairs, and stopped where he could watch from over and across the platform. He much preferred to remain a safe distance away.

Its landing was smooth and confident. When it folded its majestic wings, a light glow hopped off its back, hardly visible in sunlight. He waited. Another hawk landed without a sound, floating and settling just long enough for another light glow to hop down and disappear into the cave.

He wished Gretchen could see this. Where was she?

Luke guessed Willy might have called the clan meeting for tonight.

Gretchen climbed the stairs and stopped just a few steps below Luke. "What are you doing here?"

"Watching hawk landings and takeoffs," he reported. "We might not be able to get Willy's attention with all the activity."

A hawk floated in the distance and eyed them with suspicion. A squirrel chattered in a nearby tree. They walked across the Valley View platform and entered the cave.

"Did you ring the bell yet?" Gretchen asked.

He pulled the small brass bell from beneath his t-shirt and shook it. They waited.

Luke asked, "What errands did you run?'

"Oh, me? Just the usual," Gretchen replied, avoiding his eyes.

That was strange. Typically she was a torrent of information and details when he questioned her about something like that. "What did 'the usual' even mean?" Luke wondered.

Willy appeared, lively, alert and ready to give it a go. He pronounced, "Hello! I see you have your technology, Luke. Give me enough time to get back to Meeting Rock and we'll position your camera. Some of the boys will wait at the jagged turn to guide your camera down. Your timing is *fortuitous*." Willy winked at Gretchen. "I've been reading Dictionary."

He continued, "Shirley is serving a meal. Best way to get the others to visit, you know." Willy winked again before he continued.

"Get situated and send the line down in the same way you did the water tube and I'll make sure you get a front row seat at our gathering. How's that sound?"

Gretchen was intrigued and nearly interrupted him to ask, "What's Shirley serving?"

Willy welcomed her question and replied, "She made a clover, sorrel salad with huckleberry dressing. And there's mushroom soup, the envy of all, and of course, her acorn muffins; everyone loves those. Not sure if she managed to put together a soufflé, but we'll see! Off I go then!"

Luke was equally enthusiastic. "Thank you, Willy!" He wasted no time leaving the cave and scrambling atop the boulders, helping Gretchen up after him.

"Watch for squirrels!" Luke advised as he guided the video probe down the precipice and waited for the "gents" to direct it into their home.

Both watched with excitement as the cord was pulled into the depths of Mount Haycock. When it stopped moving, the view transmitted to Luke's smartphone took their breath. They saw, for the first time, a glimpse of the subterraneous dwelling. Luke and Gretchen marveled at the cozy home deep within the granite boulders of Earth.

The sparkle and shimmer of the rock walls reminded them of holiday lights, illuminating sparkles of pink and white quartz and red feldspar. Willy pointed the camera and light around to show off the artwork on walls, the paintings and drawings were of canoes, windmills, flowers and plants.

Tables and chairs were arranged around outcroppings of rock. Braided rugs warmed the space, made from vines and intertwined with furs and milkweed pod hairs.

When Willy panned to the origin of their water flow, he paused to show off Luke's contribution. Toppers had attached a different valve to the one provided by Dean and Luke. Their valve created a waterfall of sorts, aerating the water in sprinkles that bounced from a series of rocks before starting a journey downward.

The trickle of water glistened as it flowed over green mosses, rocks and plants. The stream ended at a tranquil pond with greenery and flowers lining its edges. Luke and Gretchen were both awed at the sight of the babbling brook, the centerpiece of their community.

Next, the camera landed on Shirley. She waved. Across the spacious opening, she stood beside a long table set with dishes and trays of food and drink. In a room behind her were cook stoves and hanging utensils, tables with bowls and other equipment used for the preparation of meals.

When Willy moved the small camera, its light revealed other rooms and residents.

Gretchen sighed when she saw a bedroom with an overstuffed, fluffy bed and a rocking chair, and she squeaked with delight when she caught a glimpse of a tiny dog strolling, tail wagging, chasing one of the Topper children.

Willy positioned the camera to give them a view of an ornate chair behind a podium. It rested upon an elevated, flat rock and was situated under a single ray of sunlight. A moment later, he took a seat in the chair.

"Willy must be sitting on Meeting Rock," Luke commented. "He looks like he's on stage. There's not much light down there. I wonder if their golden eyes help them see in the dark."

"The light on the video probe seems to be working well," added Gretchen.

Five representatives took seats in a circle before Willy. Reaching from beneath the podium, Willy removed, lifted and pounded a ceremonial gavel, calling for everyone's attention. He pronounced:

"Whereas we, Willy and Shirley of Babbling Brook Society, Barbara and Frank of Waterfall Down Lodge and Larry and Claire of Cranny Nook Circle, come together as duly elected leaders of our respective clans do hereby convene for a special meeting as set forth in Article 3 of our Rumney Constitution. We are here today for purposes of collective wellbeing and our promise to secure a safe and bountiful future for our children. To this end, I make a motion to declare friendship with two Morts: Luke and Gretchen."

Larry and Claire murmured to each other.

Barbara and Frank looked at Shirley.

Willy waited.

Luke and Gretchen were dumbstruck. Neither had any idea they were on the agenda.

Willy continued. "In the past, we have avoided interaction with Morts, with one exception: Charles. Consider how friendship with Charles helped each of us: the books which brought knowledge, a new design for bog houses, and plans for siege weapons. Each clan benefitted from our association with him."

Willy paused for their acknowledgements before resuming. "Now, it is no secret that I have established contact with the tall Mort. Barbara has met him and Larry, I know you've seen Luke around."

Barbara nodded.

Larry scowled.

"Luke is the reason we have a plentiful supply of flowing water. He and Dean, the older fellow who we've seen in the park for many years..."

Larry growled.

So loud and brash was Larry's response to the mention of Dean's name, Willy stopped and glared in his direction before continuing.

"They provided our new water source. And, bog plants were delivered by the Mort with wavy hair. Gretchen obtained the medicine which helped two of our children recover, as Shirley and Barbara can attest."

Barbara and Shirley nodded in agreement.

"Luke and Gretchen have established trust. I believe that if we are to survive the change presented now in the age of Anthropocene, we must also change. My motion is to establish friendship with them." Willy paused. "I will now recognize any member who wishes to speak."

Barbara stood and waved her hands. "Just a quick question, if I may."

Willy recognized her.

She asked, "What is that word you used to describe the age we're in? Anthropocene?"

Willy responded, "Yes, that's the word."

"Please explain," Barbara requested.

"I learned it from Dictionary, a book that has words arranged alphabetically. It provides definitions, usages and pronunciations. Fascinating reading. If you'd like to borrow it, I am happy to share when I've finished. I'm up to the letter 'g.'"

Willy waited for Barbara's response and appeared hopeful she would take him up on his offer. She was not, however, remotely interested in borrowing a book. She waved off his suggestion and indicated that *that* would not be at all necessary.

And so he continued. "Now, to the word in question. Anthropocene is the period of time we're living in now, a time of great Mort impact and climate change, which is another term recently explained to me by Luke. Climate change involves the gradual warming of the Earth. So, with that, I hope I have clarified, and again, I will now recognize any member who wishes to speak."

Barbara sat.

Larry stood and cleared his throat. "I would."

Willy said, "You have the floor."

"That Mort, Dean, he stole our artillery from the northwest tree hollow. Squirrels got me out of his evil clutches just in time. And Luke, the one you're so fond of, he ambushed John while he was on assignment for rubber loops!"

Barbara and Frank exchanged comments about Larry's charges and Claire added, "Dean is a thief and Luke is a kidnapper!"

Willy banged the gavel and yelled, "Order!"

Larry remained standing.

Willy spoke. "My question in response to your claim is this: what can you tell us about Luke's extension cable?"

Larry pointed to the cord attached to the camera probe and yelled, "That one over there? The one they're using to spy on us?"

Everyone faced the video with a variety of expressions: anger, curiosity, surprise, fear. Only Shirley smiled, which Gretchen and Luke appreciated. Larry's outburst provided a chance to see the faces of each participant. Gretchen giggled at the sight of them.

"I invited them to this meeting by way of that," Willy said calmly. "Now, let's get back to the incident with Dean. I know what Dean was after and it wasn't yours, Larry. A squirrel stole Luke's cord and you put him up to it. I will, however, ask Luke about the stolen weaponry. If it is returned to you, would that be satisfactory?"

"We want it back and it best be in good working order, is all I have to say."

"Now, back to the incident with John. What happened?" Willy asked.

"He was on a mission when Luke arrived unexpectedly, and hunted for him. When he couldn't find him, he blocked the escape route, trapping him in. John didn't return home until the next morning. Claire was beside herself with worry."

Claire put her face in hands to conceal tears and the others looked upon her with concern. When she believed she'd achieved enough sympathy, she whimpered, "It was just awful."

Willy wasn't fooled by Claire. He doubted her sincerity. Everyone in all the clans knew John was a daredevil.

Willy responded, "Well, I can speak for all of us when I say we're glad John is okay. But, his job is one that involves risk. He knew that when he signed on for it. So, it's not fair to blame Luke."

Larry was angry. "What's the point in even bringing it to a vote? Your mind appears already made up. It seems that the friendship with them has already been formalized with or without our agreement. I've heard him using the bell! Morts destroy our houses and steal from us. I won't have it!"

Claire stood beside Larry and added, "I'm with Larry! Morts are nothing but trouble."

Luke wished he could participate, to defend himself, but that was impossible. He and Gretchen exchanged uneasy looks.

Barbara stood and waived for attention.

Willy gaveled and said, "Barbara, it's your turn. Larry and Claire, take a seat."

Barbara adjusted her belt and tossed back her hair. "As you know, the kids were crazy with their latest fixation to ride beaver backs. For a while, it seemed innocent enough. But as they started to go faster and the rides got wilder, they were falling off and crashing about and gulping water from the pond. When they got sick, we gave them elderberry, blackberry and root of Echinacea teas, all our usual remedies, but Bill and Pam just weren't gettin' better. The medicine Gretchen gave us cured them. Now I don't know if their illness would have been fatal, but it might have been, and that's big. So, I think you know how I feel about Gretchen. And, Luke, well he's a fine chap, really, a bit clumsy, but his heart's in the right place. So, I'm inclined to agree with your motion, Willy."

Larry grumbled.

Claire shot her a dirty look.

Barbara continued. "That Anthropocene you spoke of, I believe it, and I agree we need help with the changes. That said, I also appreciate Larry's concerns and have a suggestion. Charles helped us with our bog houses, extending the beaver lodges and elevating them with stilts. If it wasn't for him, we certainly wouldn't be living at the pond anymore. What if Luke designed new homes for Loggers?"

The other ruminated and Barbara addressed her next comment directly to Claire. "You're grumpy because of your cramped living spaces."

"I'm not grumpy!" Claire insisted. "I'm cautious."

"You're afraid!" Barbara countered.

"Order!" Willy demanded. "Let's table the motion and give Luke and Gretchen a chance to make amends with the Loggers. Then, we'll put the declaration of friendship to a vote. It will be tabled until after the Morts respond. Will someone second this motion?"

"I second the motion," agreed Frank, happy to get a word in.

"Meeting adjourned," said Willy, smacking the gavel with robust fanfare.

Willy and Shirley both approached the video probe and waved. Willy said, "I'll be right up with some of Shirley's muffins. She wants you to taste them." Shirley continued waving and smiling.

Luke gasped. "I wish we recorded that."

"Shirley's smile and wave or the whole meeting?" asked Gretchen, but she didn't wait for Luke's reply. She knew what he meant and added, "We've recorded it in here," she said, pointing to her head, "and here," pointing to her heart.

Both sat in silence looking out across the Baker River Valley. From their vantage point above the caves, they watched as squirrels scampered to the entrance of Bear's Den. Light glows hopped on squirrel's backs and disappeared over the boulders and into the forest.

"There go the Loggers," whispered Luke.

The hawks floated to their landing spot, one at a time, collected a light glow and soared over the treetops toward the fen.

"There go the Boggers," whispered Gretchen.

Eager to get into Bear's Den to talk to Willy, Luke pulled on his cable. When it snagged, he yanked and wiggled it back and forth in an attempt to shake it loose. The jagged edges of granite were unforgiving. He jerked and tugged until it flew out and ricocheted off a boulder. Upon closer inspection, he could see that the camera lens had cracked.

"There's my lesson to slow down. Rush and regret it."

Luke and Gretchen descended with caution and entered Bear's Den where Willy stood holding a plate made of carved wood. On it were two tiny muffins, each about the size of a blueberry. "Here you go," he said.

They popped a muffin in their mouths, savored the morsel and watched each other's expression of supreme enjoyment. The texture, the flavor, the perfect blend of sweet and nutty, an aftertaste that pleaded for just one more. "Wow," Gretchen said. "Those are amazing!"

"That's why my tummy looks like it does!" Willy mused, rubbing his stomach.

"How does she make them? They've got the consistency of a moist corn muffin, the flavor of a peanut butter cookie and what's the berry flavor?"

"She'd be happy to share the recipe. The only part I help with is grinding the acorns at the mill. I know she uses two scoops of...."

Luke stopped him. "Sorry to interrupt, but you have a mill?"

"Yes we do. Our millstone was carved by my father, Drew."

"But, how is it powered?"

"It's pretty simple, really. The sails are set up on the top of the cliff. The wind shaft is made of ironwood and the great spur wheel is in our machinery room, same place we keep our steam burst equipment. The spur wheel connects to a gear wheel which turns our millstone."

"I've never seen a windmill up there."

"That's intentional," said Willy.

Luke thought for a moment and proposed, "Your windmill might be the answer to keeping the cistern from freezing in the winter. We could create a heating coil by connecting wire..."

"Hang on there, Luke. We'll use our deep Earth heated steam bursts to melt the ice. We've been melting ice ever since we got here! Remember? If you get us another tube to carry the steam to the cistern, we'll handle it."

"Right you are, Willy." Luke was relieved and ever impressed with Willy's ingenuity.

He held his finger out to Willy, a gesture which Willy understood to be the Mort custom of a greeting, or friendship or promise. Not entirely sure which one of those Luke had intended, he obliged by extending his right hand to Luke's finger. The sensation was something akin to a combination of static electricity and frostbite. Luke drew his finger back when he felt the sharp tingles.

Gretchen said, "We are honored by your motion to declare friendship with us."

"There is nothing better." Willy pronounced.

Gretchen smiled and asked, "Do you have pets? I thought I saw a black and white dog."

Willy mused, "That was Ploppy."

"Ploppy?"

"When he was a puppy, he plopped on anyone and everyone. So, we named him Ploppy. He's no longer a puppy, but the name stuck. Cute, isn't he?"

"Yes!" Gretchen concurred.

Willy turned his attention to Luke. "You heard Larry, I assume. Do you know where the Logger's artillery might be?"

"I have it. Should I bring it to you?" Luke asked.

"It's best if you return it to the hollow. The trebuchet is especially challenging to hoist. The declaration of friendship will be put up for another vote after they receive their weapons. Good evening to you both!" Willy tipped his hat, bent at the waist and scurried away.

Luke gathered his materials before heading down the path. He and Gretchen were pensive, lost in thought, amazed at the hidden society, awed by Willy's leadership and wisdom.

Lights were on at Bob's house. Neither wanted to explain why they were at the caves at this late hour. Gretchen quickened her pace, but Luke lingered. He stopped a short distance from Maple Lodge, turned around and peered up at Hawk's Cliff to catch sight of a windmill. No vanes or sails were visible.

CHAPTER 13

The errands Gretchen ran the previous day were for Luke's surprise birthday party. Colorful balloons floated from ribbons tied to a gift. Employees pitched in for *Harry Potter: The Complete 8-Film Collection (Blu-ray)*. Luke blew out candles and carved and distributed pieces of a chocolate cake, a cake in the shape of a mountain with a Happy 19th Birthday Luke banner.

How did Gretchen find out? Luke was hush hush when it came to his personal life. He finally understood when she whispered in his ear, "Remember when you asked me to snoop around the personnel files?"

After the birthday cake, Bob held a meeting to review Community Day. Admission would be free for any person showing proof of residence in either Rumney or Plymouth. He assigned stations and tasks.

Dean raised his hand. "Back in the day, my buddies and I would come to local's day with our lunch packed and buy penny candies and explore. So, that's tellin' ya how old I am, but when my father was young and he came to it, he helped make ice cream by chipping ice from the caves, adding rock salt and loading it in wooden buckets. The ladies would bring the goods and by goods I mean fresh cream, eggs, vanilla, sugar, and maybe fruit, for the best ice cream, the old fashioned way, churning it in hand-cranked wooden buckets. The kids would take turns cranking and might even fight for the chance..." Dean dramatized the churning gesture, and continued.

"That is, until they realized how tired your arm got. And my father, who loved the story about Tom Sawyer, made the cranking look like sport. And, who knows where I'm goin' with this one?"

Gretchen jumped to her feet as if on a game show and screamed, "Whitewashing the fence!"

"Right you are!" Dean exulted in her enthusiasm and participation. "He collected pennies to give up the privilege to churn the ice cream."

"We should give out free ice-cream," suggested Gretchen. The staffers agreed with the loudest approval coming from Luke who clapped his hands so hard, Danny covered his ears and gave him a look.

Bob took back the floor to wrap up the meeting. "Thank you, Gretchen and Dean. It's helpful to understand the history of this place and tell just those sort of anecdotes or really, any information about the park. I encourage you to share what you know with members of the community tomorrow. Meeting adjourned. Lots to do!"

The following day was all hands on deck for Community Day. Some guests stayed in Main Lodge to browse or watch the monitors playing Luke and Gretchen's feature film named *Polar Caves: Tales and Treks*. One woman was especially complimentary of the video and asked to speak with the general manager.

Bob introduced himself and listened as she regaled him with her many visits to the caves over the years.

"When I was a young girl, I remember guides who told some of the same stories I heard on that movie. Those boys, oh my, some were *so* good lookin'!" She jabbed her elbow into Bob's ribs.

Bob offered a courteous, manufactured smile and looked for an excuse, *any* excuse to depart, but she seemed to have cornered him. He listened politely as she rambled.

"Why metal boxes that played those recordings *ever* replaced handsome, muscular, hiker-types, real mountain men, you know, I'll just *never* understand. How is a metal speaker going to help anyone who gets stuck in the Lemon Squeeze? I ask you that."

But, she wasn't asking, really, thought Bob. She hardly took a breath between sentences and she certainly didn't pause long enough for him to offer an answer.

"One time I wedged myself in that Lemon Squeeze. Now that's a funny story. I ripped my shirt... right about here."

Bob couldn't bear to look, excusing himself with apologies. He had to check on something, a *very* pressing something, and darted away.

Gretchen distributed free ice cream and made two additional trips to Hannaford. She replenished dwindling reserves of ice cream sandwiches, the preferred treat.

Luke spent the day at Polar Ascent assisting climbers and regaling them with the history of vie ferrate. "The iron paths originated in the Dolomites, a mountain range in northeastern Italy and date back to World War One. The military used them to move troops and supplies." He must have said that twenty times throughout the day.

Dean watched kids run around, especially in Rock Garden. It was great to see them make up games and play hide-n-seek and do all the imaginative things kids liked to do when they were safe with nature, unstructured and inspired by their surroundings.

He watched from the whistle carving station he set up overlooking Rock Garden. Earlier, he'd made a stack of pre-cut, hollow dowels. When a young girl or boy approached, he beveled the fort-five degree mouthpiece and notched air holes. If they stuck around long enough to watch him finish whittling, they received a free, hand-carved whistle with instructions to "Give it a blow!"

After a few hours, whistle sounds were heard from nearly every corner of the park. A few clever children whistled back and forth with their unique tunes, communicating with each other. It sounded like a bird sanctuary.

At the end of Community Day, Luke approached Dean in the maintenance building and told him about the Topper's home, the meeting, their disagreements, how Loggers accused Dean of stealing and Luke of kidnapping, breaking the video camera probe, and Shirley's muffins.

Dean listened with the intensity of a child who hears Santa in their living room.

"How many sprites were there?" Dean wondered.

"Six attended the meeting, but we could see others walking around before it started. It was really something. Willy told me they have a windmill! If I can get them more plastic tubing, they have a cold weather solution for the cistern."

Dean pointed to a series of hooks on the wall in the workshop. "Like that one, over there? You can take it. It's leftover. Saving it for a good use," Dean said.

Luke retrieved it and asked, "Ever been on top of Hawk's Cliff?"

"Nope."

"Ever want to go?"

"No, thankee!"

"Maybe I could send a quadcopter drone up there..."

Dean interrupted him. "Okay, listen up Mr. Techie, save the drone idea for a minute. I've been thinkin', if I'm goin' up the tree again it's not gonna be just to return their weapons. I think we should build 'em a treehouse. Truth is, the idea came to me when I was up there. I know the perfect spot for it. Might need your help..."

"You got it," assured Luke, always eager to complete a project with Dean. "It is such a coincidence that you should say that. When we attended the meeting Willy called, Barbara suggested that the Loggers were grumpy, yeah, I think she said grumpy, because of their tight living quarters. They aren't happy and they need better housing."

"You know what I say about coincidences, right?"

"Yeah, the cosmic forces of the universe connect us all and are purposeful, or something like that," replied Luke.

"Close enough," Dean said, showing him pieces of wood they would use to build a small house. He also showed Luke the design he'd made.

"This is wicked cool, Dean! Let's get started."

Dean demonstrated joint construction, how to incorporate dowels and dovetails, how to reinforce block corners. Though they prided themselves in top-rate, quality construction, they also joked about their new relationship, a close bond if you will, with wood glue. "Just to be sure..." Dean would offer as justification. The house was 800 square inches, not including the generous front porch.

They worked on the Logger's house well into the night. More than once he reminded Luke to "measure twice and cut once." It was, after all, a carpenter's most important rule.

The following day, Luke delivered rubber tubing to Willy and told him about Dean's idea. He would install a treehouse as a gesture of goodwill when he returned the Logger's weapons. Willy pronounced it to be a splendid idea and showed his appreciation by way of acorn muffins, a baker's dozen. He hoisted a woven sack up and into Luke's palm with instructions. "Share those with Gretchen and Dean!"

Luke promised he would. After Dean tasted one for the first time, he asked for four more, leaving eight to be split equally between Luke and Gretchen. "You each had one before this, so it's fair! I know a baker's dozen, Luke." He popped them in his mouth one by one, to relish their rich flavor, dense consistency and earthy goodness.

The next day, it was raining and the temperature had dropped. Wind gusted every now and again. It was one of few inclement weather days they'd had that summer and rainy days meant fewer guests and a slower work day. Gretchen stopped by to monitor their progress and help when she could, always intrigued at Dean's ingenuity and skill.

She said, "I like how the roof hangs over."

"That's what you call an eave," Dean explained.

"And the columns, did you carve those?"

"Ayuh, that detail is thanks to my dad. He's the one who gave me my first chisel set and taught me to carve."

Dean reminisced. "Many a time I'd sit with him on our back porch to shape wood. We'd whittle with our pocket knives. He's the one who taught me to carve the whistles I handed out on Community Day."

Gretchen said, "Those were a huge success. The birds must have been going crazy."

"Ayuh. It was noisy for sure."

Gretchen watched as Dean put strips of wood veneer on the roof for shingles. "It reminds me of a Swiss Chalet with all the decorative trim, and what do you call these posts connected across the front porch?"

"Those are balusters. I used beech twigs," replied Dean. "I prefer veranda instead of porch. Sounds classier, don't ya think?"

"Yes, well, it's just so adorable. It reminds me of a dollhouse, only better. And, larger than I expected too, with the four rooms. Wow, look at these windows..." She peered through them.

"Luke found 'em on eBay, five of 'em. It's the decorative molding really makes stand out. So, I have a task for you." Dean placed a final shingle on the roof and walked to another workbench to show Gretchen material for curtains.

"Measure the windows and cut the fabric to size, wrap the top over and hand stitch. Here's needle and thread. These are the rods we'll put through the top and I'll hang 'em tonight."

She busied herself with cutting and sewing simple, beige curtains while Luke stained wood on the treehouse. It needed to blend in with the forest.

Gretchen told them about what she had uncovered when she researched stories about how Polar Caves were used during Prohibition. "Never found out anything specific to the caves, but I saw a lot of evidence that showed it was a complete failure. As soon as the government said you can't drink, people did it even more."

"Solution was worse than the problem," Dean said, and added, "I had a great uncle who was jailed for breakin' the law, caught selling hard cider, and when Prohibition ended, he still had six months to serve and sure enough, he had to serve those last six months. Came out as hard as that cider he was makin'."

Dean continued working on the roof and explained, "Now mind you, the Loggers will just use this as their summer place. Further up the tree is their main tree hollow, so it's important that the tree never gets cut down. Lookee here."

Dean walked to another work table and pointed to a sign he painted, similar to others around the park. It read: **Protected Tree**

Next, Dean showed off a small rain barrel fashioned from a copper, cylindrical cup. It was bolted to the roof.

Dean said, "The one thing I noticed about that Logger was dirt on his clothes, his face, so I got to wonderin', how is it that they even get clean? Wet tree hollows are few and far between, so I fashioned this rain barrel and ran a tube, like so, with a control valve above this tea cup. Should be large enough for 'em to shower or take a bath, if they're so inclined. I drilled a drain hole and used a chunk of pencil eraser for the stopper."

"That is a lovely cup. Is it fine china?" Gretchen wondered, admiring its floral and silver markings.

Dean whispered from one side of his mouth. "Found it in one of our cupboards. Hope the missus doesn't notice."

CHAPTER 14

L uke whispered the news to Gretchen when they were alone in the office. "Charles wrote back. He wants us to call him as soon as possible. His number's in the 212 area code."

"Are you going to call him?"

"That decision is up to Willy, but I am going to poke around the Internet and see what I can find out about Charles Haarin from New York City."

Luke discovered his name was linked to a business called Teeny Tomes, a publisher and printer of miniature books. He scrolled through their selection of titles.

As he perused the website, he felt his discovery might shed light on a potential conflict of interest. His gut told him Charles's motivation might be dishonorable. He should proceed with caution; trust but verify, as the Russian proverb instructed. At the end of the workday, Luke knew he needed to tell Willy *all* about Charles.

After Luke told Willy, he waited as the little guy deliberated. Luke watched, waited and noticed his teeth were surprisingly healthy for an aging elfin creature, more yellow than white, jagged and pointy, but a good looking set of choppers nonetheless. Every time Luke visited with Willy he noticed something else about him.

Willy said, "Well, I say yes to Charles's visit, and perhaps he could bring more books for my continued *enlightenment*."

"You're enjoying that dictionary!" Willy smiled and Luke continued. "Okay, I'll tell Charles you want more books and I'll bring him up to see you. But, keep in mind, people change."

"We all change, Luke."

"He won't be able to hear you, so I'll have to be a go-between."

"And I thank you for your assistance. How goes the effort to return weaponry to the Loggers?"

Luke explained that Dean would climb the tree as soon as possible and return their artillery. Luke described the treehouse in detail including methods to install it just as Dean had explained: drilling the pilot holes, installing perimeter beams and placing knee braces. "Do you think the Loggers will use it?"

"I would hope they both use it and delight in it. It may be just the thing to turn their opinion of Morts around. From your description, it sounds amazing, extraordinary, astonishing!"

"Those are called synonyms, Willy."

"Good to know. I've not reached the "s" words in Dictionary yet. Good evening, Luke!"

Luke prepared for his phone call with Charles in the Maintenance Building. He was anxious about the call. The nerves were because of the business Charles either managed or owned, the business of Teeny Tomes. He needed to find out as much as he could about it and planned the conversation in his mind. After introductions, they would talk about Willy and then his business of selling miniature books, in that order.

He dialed the number and Charles answered. Luke quickly picked up on his British accent. Charles was happy to hear that Willy had come out of hiding. Luke shared details about the park and his job before he asked Charles tell about himself:

"Well, let's see... I was born and raised in Lincolnshire, England and moved to the states to attend Dartmouth. After my junior year, a friend invited me to visit his parent's home in Holderness. The scenery was breathtaking. The water, mountains, lush landscapes, all simply bucolic. I couldn't endure leaving. Have you been there? To Squam Lake?"

"No, I haven't," responded Luke.

"Beautiful spot. Truly enchanting. It grabbed me and wouldn't let go, so captivating, ah yes..., the summer of '73..."

"I hear it's nice out there," Luke was compelled to fill in the extended pause with something.

Charles continued, "As it happened, there was a small apartment above the boat house for lease. If I could secure employment, I would live there. My friend worked at the park, so I applied. Got the job and worked as a guide under the tutelage of David."

Luke asked, "How did you meet Willy?"

"Ah yes, the little man. I had a habit of climbing up and lingering on some of the higher rock formations. Liked the view. One day I saw a glow of light and I reached for it. Thought, perhaps, it was an immense lightning bug. In reaching for the glow I knocked a stone and the glow turned into a little person. Bloody marvelous, I thought... found an elf! It was William."

Luke retold of his initial encounter with Willy and Charles laughed. "Ha! Your first meeting reminds me of my own. When I met the cheeky bugger, he was utterly uncivilized. Dirty clothes, a bit savage, shirty."

"Shirty?" asked Luke.

"Oh sorry, short-tempered. And he spoke French which, by luck, I had studied in my secondary school, so I was able to converse. That summer I taught him English. I met him every day at sunrise, rain or shine. Willy is smart, extremely astute, have you noticed?"

"Very intelligent," agreed Luke.

"He learned the alphabet in two minutes, heard it and recited it perfectly, had an exceptional ability to hear things once and remember. I instructed him in etiquette and rules of order. Most important, don't you think?"

Luke remembered the quote Willy recited and repeated it. "Life be not so short but that there is always time for courtesy."

"Ralph Waldo Emerson. You heard that from Willy, didn't you?"

"And he said he learned it from you."

"Amazing recall, that little elf. After he learned English, we concentrated on manners. He wanted to understand how our society worked and our customs. He really took to science too, loved all things mechanical especially. Did he tell you about the deep Earth steam bursts configuration?

"He did, at our very first meeting, actually." Luke could have offered details about the cistern, but he was hesitant to reveal too much, still wary of whether Charles could be trusted.

Charles continued. "I must say, he craved any and all instruction I offered, very motivated, soaked it like a sponge. Over time I began to think of him as more than just an amazing new species of gnome. More than just a student. He was like my adopted child, well, except for the fact that he was so much older."

"How old is he?"

"I don't know. I'm not sure he even knows. It was difficult for me to keep up with his demand for reading material, but I wanted to provide whatever I could. It was hard to find miniature books, but I located a few: Dickens and Tolkien."

That was it. Luke's chance. "What can you tell me about Teeny Tomes?"

Charles said nothing. After a pause, he responded. "Done your research have you?"

Luke thought, ha! If you're so concerned with etiquette, Charles, you should know it's not polite to answer one question with another. Luke was proud of himself for posing the question and he waited. When it became uncomfortably obvious that Charles was not inclined to say more, he probed further. "Do you *own* the business?"

"Well, yes. It's rather a side-business, hardly profitable. You might call it more of a hobby. Not much demand, if you will. Haven't updated the website in some time."

Their conversation was nearing its awkward end. Before making arrangements for a visit, which was exactly what Charles wanted now that Willy Topper had "come out of hiding," as he put it, Luke had more questions. "Who came up with the clan names?"

"Ah yes, that was after I taught him the British custom to name a manor house. One could name it based upon people living in it or for its unique features. The little people adored the tradition and made up the names. Willy was such a clever bloke; I do miss him."

"Why did your friendship end? He said you went deaf, but that's obviously not true."

"At the end of the season, I told David I wanted to return the next summer and again work as a guide. He thanked me for my dedicated service, praised me for arriving early every day of the week, even on my days off. He gave me a cash bonus, actually. Much appreciated. He also explained that he would not need my services next year. Guides were being replaced with devices, the technology of the day. Press a button and a pre-recorded message would play. Self-guided was the term then. I was offered another position on the grounds, but that wouldn't have been the same.

When I told Willy, he nearly cried. I promised to come back the following year, and I did. I stayed at 'our spot' for as long as I could, but Willy never appeared. I called for him over and over and waited. No sign of him. That summer I moved to New York City, so it became harder for me to visit and at that point, I thought Willy was gone."

Luke knew he needed to extend an invitation then. He had a deeper appreciation for Willy's desire to see Charles. Their association had been pivotal to Willy and his community, had changed their views of the world, opened doors for the Toppers. Luke also wanted to have more conversations with Charles. He had many unanswered questions about the Boggers and Loggers. "Whenever you can make it here, I'll take you to Willy. He wants to see you."

Charles exclaimed, "Bloody marvelous! I'll drive up on Saturday and text you when I arrive. I'm chuffed!

"Chuffed?" asked Luke.

"Excited!" Charles returned. "See you Saturday!"

While Luke was talking to Charles, Dean had entered the workshop and busied himself organizing his tools, but as soon as Luke terminated the call, he probed for information without a word. He just stopped what he was doing and stared.

Luke said, "That was Charles. He's coming on Saturday."

"That's the day after tomorrow," reminded Dean.

"He's eager. I guess it makes sense. Weekends are probably when he's not working."

"What does he do?"

"I'm not sure, but he owns a miniature book business and says it's a hobby." Luke leaned against a table as if he needed the support.

Dean watched his friend, unsure of whether to tell him what he thought about the visit from Charles or if he should just change the subject. He did both.

"Ayuh, always good to see a former guide. It's been a long time. Now, let's talk about how we're gonna install this treehouse."

The plan was this: Dean would ascend and Luke would load a canvas tote attached to a pulley system. He would hoist the weaponry, supports and treehouse. Dean would have his tools with him on the climb and whatever wouldn't fit in his tool belt he would stow in his backpack.

Luke practiced pulling the cord through a grooved rim of the pulley wheel when Bob entered and asked, "How goes it?"

Surprised by his entrance, Luke stuttered, "Good, ah, just on my way to update our SharePoint site and the firewall needs tweaking and..." As he headed out of the workshop, he glanced backwards and winked. He couldn't resist. "Nice dollhouse, Dean!"

Dean stood before the miniature treehouse and greeted Bob with his usual friendly demeanor. "What's up boss?"

"I should ask the same of you. What have you got there?"

"This?" Dean stepped beside to allow Bob a full view of the quaint house with its wraparound deck, decorative windows and pitched roof.

"Why are you making a dollhouse?"

"It's for squirrels," clarified Dean.

"You built a house for squirrels?" Bob approached it. "How are they going to open the front door?"

"Clever critters. Best to never underestimate them."

"It looks like it was designed by Frank Lloyd Wright," observed Bob.

"Why thank you. I prefer to chalk it up to Yankee ingenuity."

"Seems a shame to give it to the squirrels. I have a granddaughter who would love to put her Kelly dolls in it."

"Kelly dolls?" Dean was not familiar.

"You know Barbie?"

"Ayuh."

"They're Barbie's small friends."

"I can make another for her. It was loads of fun and I used scrap wood, odds and ends." Dean quickly showed him the features and suggested improvements he would incorporate when he made one for Bob's granddaughter."

"Oh, she'd love it. It would be the perfect Christmas gift for her, that is, if you can manage it. Don't want you to go out on a *limb*, so to speak."

Dean didn't react. He grew suspicious. Did Bob know he planned to install it in on a *tree limb*? A squirrel box was usually connected to the side of a tree trunk, about thirty feet up.

Bob changed the topic. "The stone delivery is here."

"I'll head right over," Dean informed, walking to the door.

"Make sure they give you the invoice. Last time they billed us nine months after delivery and it messed up our accounting."

"You got it." Dean darted out to meet the contractor and Bob remained, admiring the small house.

Bob appreciated the running water arrangement and puzzled how a squirrel would *ever* be clever enough to turn a valve like the one Dean had installed.

CHAPTER 15

Charles arrived at Polar Caves, parked his car and slowly climbed the wide stairs. He sat on a bench just outside Main Lodge and looked around as if committing the layout to memory. When he entered the lodge, he was neither prepared nor interested in purchasing a ticket to enter the park. He wasn't doing anything disruptive or illegal, but he caught Bob's attention.

Bob asked if he could be of any assistance and Charles replied with a polite, "No, thank you. Just browsing." He used the restroom twice and paced the floors for nearly an hour, picking up an item now and again.

Charles had a tidy, casual appearance. He wore a white golf shirt and beige cargo shorts. Neither had a hint of wrinkle. His boots were a rugged design, yet they gleamed with polish and shine. He wore a wide-brimmed bucket hat that matched his too neat cargo shorts. His socks were folded with a cuff and too white. A large waist pack was so flawless, it looked as if it might have the price tag still attached.

When Charles asked Bob if a fellow by the name of Luke was available, Bob was relieved and curious and yes, Bob would be happy to get him.

Luke arrived and extended his hand. Charles was a foot shorter than Luke and weighed at least fifty pounds more.

"Let's take a seat over there," suggested Luke pointing to the solid wood tables and chairs at the back of the lodge. "Why didn't you text me?"

Charles replied, "I just wanted to get the lay of the land, so to speak. No harm. Are you ready to take me up?"

"Did you buy a ticket?"

"I didn't bring any money, falling a bit short these days," explained Charles.

"Did you at least bring books for Willy?" wondered Luke.

"Yes, I have them right in here. He patted the purse attached to his waist."

"Can I see them?"

"I'd rather surprise you at the same time as Willy, if that's alright. Let's head up then, shall we?" Charles prompted.

A mild irritation brewed. Luke scoffed, "Hang on. I need to make a story up about you. I wish you would have just texted me like you said you would."

Luke explained to Bob that Charles was a quirky, distant cousin visiting from England and Bob assured him that it was no problem and approved a complimentary pass to visit the caves.

They lingered in the animal park. Charles noticed changes and pointed them out. He wondered, "What happened to the peacock? He was my favorite."

Luke replied, "Not here anymore." They walked through the covered bridge and ascended the path.

"That's new," Charles said, pointing to Maple Lodge.

There was a lot about Charles that unnerved Luke, but he tried to keep an open mind for Willy's benefit. He bolted along and up the walkways, stopping frequently for Charles to catch up. Luke watched Charles finally reach Valley View platform; his face red and dripping with sweat. Charles stood gasping for breath and Luke worried he might have some condition that would require immediate medical attention.

"Are you okay?" Luke asked.

"Fine. Just need a moment," he wheezed, pronouncing each word with a second or two in between. Charles sat on a bench to recover while Luke meandered toward Bear's Den and rang the bell to summon Willy. He was certain Charles didn't see him and equally confident he wouldn't be able to hear the bell.

"How do you get his attention?" Charles asked when he was able to speak.

"I just call for him like this. Wi–lly!"

"He hears that? All the way over here?"

"Yup," replied Luke.

Charles was breathing normally again. "Ah yes, my old stomping ground. I used to wait for Willy down there. This is a new platform and a better view. I like it. Should we head into the cave?"

"After you," said Luke, secretly ringing the bell again.

Charles struggled to get into the cave and find a comfortable position, but finally he settled in the spot where Luke directed him. They sat beside one another and Luke pointed to the opening where Willy would emerge.

"So, now, we wait?" Charles had just asked the question when Willy appeared.

"Hello Charles!" Willy raised both hands, reaching and stretching as if he wished he could grow to the size of a Mort. His wide smile conveyed joy at the sight of Charles.

Though Charles couldn't hear what Willy said, he recognized the little man's delight. He remembered his smile and those twinkling eyes. Words weren't necessary to communicate his delight.

Charles said, "He hasn't changed a bit! Not a bit!" He brought his hands to his mouth and shook his head, relieved and thrilled to see his little friend.

"You, however, have changed considerably, my friend," Willy said.

"What did he say?" asked Charles.

Luke repeated Willy's comments to Charles and added, "How could Willy not change at all in forty years?"

Charles replied, "Perhaps it is the cold temperatures in which he lives. They may preserve him and lengthen his lifespan. That would be my guess."

Luke pondered this as he aided Charles and Willy with their conversation, repeating what Willy said to Charles. Willy told Charles about his concerns regarding climate change and how Luke had helped. He explained why the Toppers switched transport from ducks to hawks and how Bogger children had become ill and recovered.

Charles posed question after question, preferring to hear all about Willy rather than telling Willy anything about himself.

Luke grew weary of the one sided conversation and said, "Willy wants to know if you brought more books."

Charles stalled. "Yes, but before we get to that, tell me Willy, how did you manage without books for all these years? It seems you have continued learning."

Willy answered his question and again waited as Luke restated his response to Charles. "Willy said, they observe Morts, watching and listening. Toppers bring information back to the community and over time, they've collected new information. But, books are much preferred." Luke pressed again, "He's ready for the books you brought."

Charles unzipped his waist pack, reached inside and pointed something directly into Luke's curious, wide eyes. It was pepper spray. Charles squeezed the trigger and continued spraying until Luke scrambled out of the cave screaming that his eyes were on fire. He coughed and groaned with pain.

Willy stood frozen in stunned disbelief. Why would his old friend hurt his new friend? He didn't understand.

Charles grabbed the unsuspecting little man and was suddenly reminded of the sting from Willy's electrical charge. He held tight to the struggling elf, pushed him into a wide-mouth Mason jar, placed a lid atop in which he had punctured holes, and screwed down the outer band.

Willy screamed for help and pounded his fists on the glass. Charles returned the Mason jar to his waist pack and zipped it mostly closed. He didn't want his old friend to suffocate. Charles exited from the other end of the cave and started his cautious descent.

Luke couldn't see. Tears filled his inflamed, burning eyes and he feared his vision would be forever damaged. Panicked with the thought of going blind, his every breath, each gasp of air that mixed with the irritant, grew more torturous.

He heard Willy's muffled cries for help and knew he must act quickly if he was going to save him. Overcoming the pain, he grabbed the bell and rang it over and over again, desperate and frantic, until he heard Shirley's familiar voice. "Luke, what happened?"

Luke choked out the words. "Charles took Willy. He needs our help. We have to stop him. He has Willy!"

"Oh dear, oh my," Shirley yelled in what sounded squeakier than usual.

"Someone needs to stop Charles!" Luke pleaded.

"Will you be alright?" Shirley had never seen a Mort in such a state of distress.

"Yes, go! Get help!"

Luke controlled his breathing to listen as Shirley screeched in alternating pitches and irregular patterns. He heard the answering cry of a hawk.

When the noises subsided, he called out, "Shirley? Shirley?" There was no answer.

The noise of the squirrels began. Luke heard the chattering "chee, chee, chee." Their alarm calls rang from the forest below.

Animals were coming to Willy's rescue. Get him. Get him. Luke chanted. Get him. Get him. His anger raged and he scolded himself for ever trusting Charles.

Luke rubbed his eyes, the worst thing he could do. Rubbing them opened his capillaries, increased the burning sensation and further spread the pain.

Two hikers approached and found Luke sitting outside the cave, blubbering, rocking back and forth in agony. His eyes were closed, the skin around them, bright red.

"Can we help you?" one asked.

His gaze was a tormented squint, the white of his eyes having turned red. When he tried to speak, he found that his throat had filled with mucous and he could only cough out one word. "Water."

A cold plastic bottle was placed into his hand. He drank from it and poured water down his face. "Could you deliver a message? It's urgent!"

"Yes," they replied in unison, eager to assist the suffering young man in whatever way they could.

"Go to the maintenance building. Ask for Dean. Tell him to stop Charles. He has a Topper."

"Dean in maintenance," one repeated.

The other confirmed, "Stop Charles. He has a Topper."

Luke added, "Tell him to look for the purse."

"Look for a purse?" they clarified.

"Yes! Charles, a Topper, in the purse. Hurry!" he urged.

Luke crawled to the bench on Valley View platform and doused his eyes with the remaining water from a plastic bottle given to him by a kind stranger.

The water helped, but he still couldn't see. Salty tears streamed down his cheeks.

CHAPTER 16

Charles walked down the path looking behind him, from left to right every few steps. Outwardly, he appeared relaxed, but inside his heart was pounding.

Willy banged against the inside of the Mason jar. When he wasn't knocking on the glass, he was rocking it back and forth. Charles didn't want any harm to befall Willy, but he also didn't dare remove his beloved prize.

Two hikers in top-notch, physical shape nearly knocked him over as they ran past. With every slow, controlled step closer to his car, Charles believed his plan would work.

Before reaching the covered bridge, without warning, he felt a sharp sting. Acorns flew through the air, one after another. More hit him. One in the head, another in the neck, two on his arm.

Acorns were flying through the air and he knew exactly who was to blame. He never like those Loggers, not one bit, and had only helped them long ago as a favor to Willy. Somehow, someone had tipped them off. He quickened his pace.

On the path along the pond, another barrage of acorns were launched. These hurt even more, hurled from a closer range. He dodged some, but when one hit him directly in the face, on the nose to be precise, he stumbled and nearly fell.

His pace accelerated. They could injure him, indeed they were doing a good job of it, but Loggers couldn't stop him. He would get Willy into his car and be gone in five minutes.

Without a moment's hesitation, Dean ran from the hikers who communicated Luke's urgent message. He looked up and down the path and spotted a man walking quickly and stiffly towards the exit. The man was on a mission. He almost didn't even need to see his face.

Still, Dean approached from behind, ran alongside and looked. Though it had been many years since Dean had seen Charles, one look was all he needed. Dean never forgot a face. It was Charles, alright.

"Well, well, well. If it isn't Charles Haarin."

Charles stopped in his tracks. "Do I know you?" he asked.

"Used to." Dean stood before the intruder. "I'm Dean. Whatcha got there?" He pointed to the pack around his waist.

"Personal items."

"Is that so? I'm gonna need you to show me those items in the office. Come with me." Dean moved abreast and grabbed his arm with a forceful nudge.

Charles turned and kicked. His steel-toe boot crashed into Dean's shin with such force, Dean doubled over and released his hold on Charles, a cry of pain echoing across the park.

When Bob heard Dean's yelp, he bolted outside to help him. He ran over to where Dean was sitting on the ground holding his leg.

Dean gushed, "The guy Luke was with, he assaulted me and Luke! You need to stop him."

Bob didn't waste a minute. First he ran into his office, then through the lodge and out the front door.

At the same time, Charles scurried down the maintenance road toward the parking lot. He couldn't run for fear of hurting Willy, but he walked as quickly as he could and as he was about to reach for his car door handle, he felt a hard poke in the middle of his back.

"I don't want to shoot you, but I will if you don't come with me."

Charles froze when the blunt object pressed into his back. He turned around and saw the general manager.

"You can't detain me. I haven't done anything wrong." Charles sneered.

"You assaulted two of my employees. You can walk with me or we can wait here for the police. Your choice. Either way, you're *not* getting in a car."

Bob led Charles up the stairs, through the lodge and into the office. He had a grip on Charles' arm, a stun gun pressed into his back.

Dean was waiting for them. When he saw Charles, Dean said, "Take off your purse and put it on the table." Irritation pulsed through each word. "Sit." Dean pointed to a chair and waited until Charles sat.

Hobbling over to Bob, Dean explained. "He smashed my shin bone and sprayed Luke with mace."

Bob was furious and approached Charles with his fist drawn, threatening, ready to punch him, but reconsidered. Instead, he turned to Dean and asked, "Should I check on Luke?"

Dean appreciated his protection, but stopped him and said, "No, I'll head up. But, keep him here," nodding in the direction of Charles. "I think Gretchen is with Luke. I'm not going to press charges, but I can't say the same for Luke. Let's hold off calling the cops until I get back. And I'll need to take this with me."

Dean lifted the waist pack from the table, gave Charles a hostile stare and left the office.

Bob pulled a chair over and sat before Charles, Taser at the ready.

When Dean arrived at Valley View, Gretchen had an arm around Luke's shoulder, comforting him. Luke sat with his head down, a bottle of water in one hand and the other shielding his swollen eyes.

"Whoa, you look bad, dude. Really bad," Dean said.

"It feels like my eyeballs are bubbling in acid," Luke said, straining to see. "What happened?"

"Charles is in the office. Bob detained him and I've got the little guy right here," he said, patting the waist pack.

"Thank God." Luke relaxed for the first time since the calamity, leaning against a chair back. "Is he okay?" Luke asked.

Gretchen watched as Dean unzipped the pack and lifted the Mason jar. Willy shook his head as if awakening from a bad dream. He looked through the thick glass at the large blurry faces and when he recognized Dean, he waved to him and wobbled to a standing position. Dean nodded back.

"What a relief," sighed Gretchen.

"Let me see him, Dean." Luke's eyes didn't appear capable of sight, but Dean obliged. Dean held Willy up before Luke's face, just inches away, and scanned the area for nearby visitors, ever cautious of passersby.

Willy yelped, "What did he do to you, Luke?"

"Pepper spray," replied Luke. "I'm so sorry, Willy."

"Don't *you* apologize! Charles is the guilty one. He is *not* the friend he once was."

"Are you okay?" Luke asked.

"Had a rough ride, but I'll be fine."

Willy smiled at Dean and offered an appreciative nod. No words were necessary between them; both understood that Willy needed to be returned to the safety of his cave.

Dean walked to the cave, opened the glass prison and watched Willy scoot up and out, onto the rock ledge leading to his home. Before Willy disappeared into the crevice, he held up a finger, and gestured for Dean to wait."

Dean understood and sat down in the familiar cave. He checked the large purple and black bruise growing on his shin. He touched it gingerly and cringed, fuming at the thought of Charles sitting in the office. He doubted Luke would press charges for the same reason he wouldn't press charges. Both cared more about protecting Toppers than they cared about teaching Charles a lesson.

Willy returned with a tiny roll of beech bark, tied with a strand of thin string. He lifted and presented it to the Mort who rescued him from the confines of a Mason jar and a waist pack.

Dean used his thumb and index finger to accept the tiny item, untied the string, and unrolled the paper thin bark. On the white background, he read *Thank You* in elaborate handwriting. Willy's message was one of the most considerate, unique notes he'd ever received; he would save it always. Dean smiled and held the scroll to his chest. Willy nodded a last time and bowed before disappearing into his dark, safe, underground world.

It took about an hour before Luke could see well enough to descend the cave trails, but even then, it was with Gretchen's help. As they walked, Gretchen explained what had happened from her perspective.

"I saw a commotion and when Dean ran past, he pointed at two hikers and told me to talk to them. I ran over and introduced myself. Their names were Sam and Michael and they said someone had been maced. Their description matched you and I assumed it must have something to do with Charles when they said you were outside of Bear's Den.

"What are we going to do?" Luke couldn't think clearly.

"I know exactly what we're going to do. The idea came to me the moment I saw Willy in that glass jar with his tools scattered around, his cap off, hair tousled and his arms pressed against the sides. I thought, my God, he's lucky to be alive. I have the perfect solution." Gretchen whispered her idea in Luke's ear.

When they got to the office, Bob welcomed Luke with a bottle of saline solution and instructions. "Take this into the restroom and flush your eyes. One of us will drive you home or take you to urgent care, whatever you think is best. Then, we'll decide what to do with Mr. Haarin."

"Let me treat the symptoms here. I'll be right back." Luke accepted the first aid from his boss.

Gretchen scrutinized Charles and scowled at him. She walked beside Luke to guide him and offer whatever help he might need.

When they returned, Bob met them in the doorway and pulled Luke aside.

He whispered, "Do you want to press charges?"

"No," Luke replied, placing a cold paper towel compress to his eyes. "I just want to talk to him."

"You're sure?" Bob persisted.

"I'm sure," confirmed Luke. "Alone, if that's okay."

"Sure. Well, since it's a family matter of sorts, I'll let you talk in private, but as soon as you're finished, I want him out of here. He is no longer welcome. Do we agree on that?"

"Completely," said Luke.

"I'll be right outside the door." Bob lifted his Taser, reminding them all that he would use it if he needed to, reluctant to depart.

"Is that a stun gun?"

"Totally legal," Bob assured him. He supposed there was something more going on, but he thought better of pressing the matter or saying anything else. Instead, he closed the office door behind him after Luke and Gretchen had entered.

Charles was disheveled and his red nose looked particularly unpleasant. His posture was horrid and with his hat removed, Gretchen and Luke could see his balding head. When Charles arrived he had the appearance of an arrogant, self-important gentleman and now he looked like a miserable, pathetic scoundrel.

Luke paced the room and Gretchen stood with her arms folded across her chest. Luke didn't speak for a few minutes (for dramatic effect, as Gretchen had suggested) before he proceeded with their plan. When it became obvious that Charles was growing uneasy, squirming in his seat, Luke blurted, "You killed him!"

"What? He's dead? But, how?" Charles stammered. "It was the Loggers. They were hitting me with nuts and made me trip. It was the Loggers who killed him."

"You cannot be serious! You're actually blaming *them* for his death?" Luke was incredulous.

"I never meant to hurt him." Charles started to cry. His lips quivered. He wiped sweat from his face.

"Why did you kidnap him?" Gretchen hissed.

"Or betray him like that?" Luke scolded.

Charles's shoulders shuddered with a pathetic display of grief.

Gretchen and Luke watched him, disgusted.

"We're waiting," Gretchen said, intent to let him know that his antics were having zero effect on their compassion or understanding. Finally, Charles began his explanation.

"I wasn't always like this. I helped Willy. We were friends."

Gretchen offered him a box of tissues. Charles accepted them and pulled one after another from the box.

"*I* am a Professor of Anthropology. *I* defended my dissertation with distinction in 1983. *I* have twenty-three published works to my name. But, of late, things haven't been as fruitful. Field research has yielded nothing of value, and it was my hope that Willy would be my ticket, my golden artifact, so to speak.   Do you know how much pressure professors are under?

"I can only imagine," said Luke dryly.

"In my discipline, discovering Willy is like finding a unicorn. It changes everything! He's the reason I went into this field and I always believed I would see him again, or one of his kind. I needed him, not a story or a photo, to prove the existence of his species. When you told me he resurfaced, I knew it was my chance. Without him I will never get the recognition I deserve."

"You deserve?" Luke blurted out and caught himself. He lowered his voice. "You just thought you could borrow him? You've made an awful mess. And for what? To satisfy your own selfish desires?"   Luke glared at Charles, but Charles wouldn't meet his gaze.

"Shame on you," Gretchen rebuked. "The only thing you deserve is jail time. You robbed the world of a priceless treasure, a beloved leader, one who can *never* be replaced."

Luke said, "Tell you what we're going to do." He walked around Charles a few times before continuing. "You're going to leave and never come back and *never* tell anyone about Willy or *any* of the other little people who live in these parts. And for that, I won't press charges. How's that sound?"

"Fair," Charles replied sadly. He blew his nose and cringed when his hand touched his wound. He stood, eyes downcast and skulked from the office.

Luke and Gretchen watched him leave the lodge and walk down the stairs. They watched him exit the parking lot and didn't stop looking until they saw his car disappear down Route 25.

As they left the window, Gretchen spotted Sam and Michael browsing in the gift shop. They held an array of items: a t-shirt, sweatshirt, a coffee mug. "Luke, those are the two that helped you today. Sam! Michael!"

They waved at Gretchen and walked over. Luke extended his hand and said, "Thank you so much. You really saved the day."

"We were happy to help. You okay?" asked Sam.

"I'll be alright. At least my vision is returning," Luke replied. "Let me put it this way, it feels as bad as it looks."

Luke stood speechless with Sam and Michael, unable to manage any conversation. He was still shaken from the day's events. Gretchen excused herself and asked them to wait just a second. She would be right back. They watched her confer with Bob.

Bob walked over and introduced himself. He said, "Sam, Michael, thank you for visiting Polar Caves Park. It's a real pleasure to meet two such service-minded individuals. To show our appreciation for your help today, I'd like to compensate you with those items. No charge."

CHAPTER 17

As the end of August approached, goldenrod bloomed and the Black-eyed Susans lining Luke's front walk started to droop. Relaxing on a lounge chair in his back yard, he spotted what looked like a hawk.

He peered through his binoculars and saw the large bird floating and gliding through the clear sky. Its flight was similar to a hawk, but the wings had a different shape. Consulting his field guide, he identified it as a Peregrine Falcon, with its white underside and tapered wings. He logged a sighting on the Audubon app.

Auspicious, he thought, to see the falcon. It was a spectacular bird. The falcon was making a comeback, now labeled as threatened, according to Audubon, and lucky to be the offspring of ancestors who survived widespread pesticide use.

He listened to its screechy call, and thought it sounded like "hurry up, hurry up." Exactly. Hurry up and give us back our habitat, our pristine lands, our home.

Bob insisted he take a few days off after the pepper spray incident. Dean visited twice with his guitar to rehearse "Wish You Were Here." Both agreed it sounded great, not particularly because their playing was flawless, but how could it not? It was a classic.

Luke saw six of the seven Harry Potter movies, promising to save the last one until Gretchen could watch it with him. When he wasn't playing guitar or watching Harry fight the most powerful wizard of all time, Luke was working on a gift, his departing gift for Willy.

Rummaging through his box of outdated technology, he found an Apple iPod nano (16 GB). He restored it to factory settings and uploaded all the Harry Potter audio books, numbering the books with separate icons to make it easy for Willy to select them in order. The iPod nano would provide about twenty hours of play time before the battery was drained. Two problems needed to be addressed. Luke needed to extend the battery life and he needed to control Willy's electrical output.

A portable battery charger would recharge the iPod four more times, an arrangement to give Willy the ability to listen to five of the seven books. It wasn't perfect, but it was the best he could manage.

If Willy was going to use the iPod's touch screen, Luke would need to protect the device from Willy's inherent charge. It would be of little use if he fried it.

Luke visited a leather shop and consulted with the owner who sold him paper-thin sheepskin that was well-suited for what he would make. Luke cut out and sewed together a tiny pair of leather mittens for Willy. It required a great deal of patience, but Luke persevered until the gloves were sewn. He wove in a single strand of stainless steel metal thread. Hopefully, Willy's electric current would be controlled by the mittens, allowing just the right amount of output by way of the metal thread.

Luke couldn't remember ever being as excited to give a gift as he was with this. Gretchen was equally thrilled when he told her what he'd arranged.

Three days after the visit from Charles and the night before Luke planned to return for his last day of work, he met Dean at Serenity Shelter.

This was the night they would give the Loggers a proper home. Together they would install the treehouse. Luke gazed up at the towering white pine tree and could see neither the hollow nor the branch to support the small house from where he stood. "Are you sure these are the right trees?" he asked, a rhetorical question that Dean ignored.

Dean checked each component of his climbing gear for safety and began his ascent. He was nearly fifty feet up the tree when he rigged a pulley and sent down a rope with a hook at one end. Luke attached the treehouse and hoisted it. He listened as Dean drilled and hammered and whistled as he worked.

"Don't forget to put their weapons back," yelled Luke.

"Already did."

Dean returned to firm ground and removed his climbing hardware. "Should we practice again tonight? You're really gettin' the hang of that G, E, A chord progression."

Luke laughed when Dean exaggerated the strumming of an air guitar and attempted lyrics. "Sorry. I promised to watch the last Harry Potter movie with Gretchen tonight. Thanks anyway."

"When do you head back to college?" Dean asked.

"Tomorrow," Luke replied. "The summer flew by."

"Always does," agreed Dean, walking on the trail behind Luke as the sun began its descent.

CHAPTER 18

The next afternoon, Luke headed up the trails with his gifts for Willy. Gretchen would be look out. Luke needed uninterrupted time to explain the iPod setup and functionality to Willy; he didn't want to worry about an approaching hiker. She sat upon Raven's Roost while Luke summoned Willy from his usual spot and waited.

When Willy arrived, he danced a jig of sorts and Luke smiled from ear to ear. Both were healthy and happy after the traumatic events and each had an abounding sense of relief.

Luke said, "I have something for you." Willy jumped back as Luke presented and opened his backpack. Luke noticed and said, "Don't worry. It's nothing like what Charles had."

Willy's apprehension was understandable.

Luke took special care to explain the array of gifts. After the comprehensive overview, Willy put on the gloves. They fit surprisingly well.

With fingers, arms and legs crossed for good luck, Luke watched his little friend give it a go.

Willy moved the iPod so that it leaned against the granite wall. He pushed his gloved hand against the icon labeled HP #1 and when the triangle appeared, he pressed play. No signs of any sizzling or popping!

Standing a few inches from one of the earbuds, Willy listened briefly and paused the recording. Willy repeated the first sentence aloud. *"Mr. and Mrs. Dursley, of number four, Privet Drive, were proud to say that they were perfectly normal, thank you very much."*

Willy exclaimed, "Oh Luke, I like it already! Though the narrator reminds me a bit of Charles." His eyes widened at the familiarity.

"Right, well, the author and the narrator are both Brits, so it's to be expected. There are seven books." Luke showed him a few more features: rewind, fast forward, bookmark, volume control.

Luke repeated the instruction, "When the battery icon turns red, you need to charge it, so that's what the battery pack is for. Try it." Luke admired Willy's dexterity as he connected the charger cord to the iPod.

Willy pointed to the battery charger. "That holds electricity?"

Luke said, "Yes, it'll recharge the iPod three or four more times. But, I don't know if you'll be able to finish all the books with it. You might have to wait until I return next year."

"The gents and I are handy when it comes to the transfer of charges. We have a room below with our collection of star stones and other rocks and minerals we've extracted. When we experiment, we like to call it 'controlling our sparks' and I think we might be able to spark the energy from the windmill to this charger. Worth a few experiments, I would say."

"That sounds amazing, Willy. I'll be interested to know if you get that to work. Maybe next year we can set things up to communicate with each other," Luke suggested.

"Brilliant! This technology is life-changing and I wonder, will Morts use technology to fix climate change?"

Luke thought for a long moment before responding. "We can only hope."

Willy gathered his gifts one by one and took them into the hidden paths of his cave dwelling. Luke waited, pleased to spend as much time as he could with his wise, joyful little friend. After Willy stowed the last of the items, he asked, "Is Gretchen here? I have something for both of you."

Peeking out from the cave, Luke waved Gretchen over. She ducked, crouched and sat beside Luke. Willy held three tiny goblets and a carafe of yellow liquid. He filled the goblets and instructed his dear friends to each take one.

"A toast, to the declaration of friendship with Luke and Gretchen. May it endure. Cheers!" Willy held up his goblet and poured the contents into his mouth. He uttered an appreciative sign and watched for Luke and Gretchen's reaction to the toast and the drink.

Gretchen and Luke looked into each other's surprised eyes, lifted their cups and poured what amounted to less than a teaspoon.

Luke spoke first. "That was some drink! Smooth and sweet, like a drop of lemon honey with a boost of warmth. And our friendship was formalized? We're truly honored."

Gretchen nodded in agreement, her eyes still wide with wonder at the flavor and heat from the liquid. "What was that?" she asked.

"Cloudberry wine. Do you like it?"

"It's wonderful! Cloudberry? I've never heard of it."

"It grows around the bog. They're about this big." Willy held his hands to show them its size which coincidentally and comically matched the dimensions of Willy's tummy. "The drupelets form to make a shape similar to a fluffy cloud, so perhaps that is why Morts named them cloudberries. When the berries are over-ripe, we crush and soak them in our oak barrels where the juice remains until it develops a tart, creamy finish. Our ancestors made cloudberry wine; it's a recipe we've perfected over many generations."

"What is a drupelet?" Gretchen asked.

Willy smiled, "That's a new word for me, too, Gretchen. According to Dictionary, it refers to the subdivisions that make up the outer layer of the berry."

Willy held the decanter to offer Gretchen and Luke another taste. They eagerly accepted. Willy poured and they each downed another glass. He collected their vessels and reached behind him for a bell similar to the one Luke wore around his neck. "This is for you, Gretchen." He handed her the miniature bell.

"Thank you, Willy! I love it." Gretchen rung it and wished she could give Willy a hug. That wasn't possible, so she blew him a kiss and crossed her arms about her chest and smiled. He understood.

Luke asked, "Did everyone approve our friendship?"

Willy explained. "Loggers visited earlier today. They were most grateful for the return of their weapons and awed by the new arrival of the treehouse. No Mort has ever done anything like that before and it turned their opinion around. They voted to declare friendship."

"And the Boggers?" Gretchen wondered.

"Unanimous agreement," assured Willy.

Gretchen lifted her finger to her ear and pointed outside the cave. Hikers were approaching. Willy quickly tipped his cap and said, "Good-bye!" Luke pointed his finger and waited for a shock of electrical charge from Willy's extended hand. Willy zapped him, bowed, turned and disappeared into the cave.

The hikers waited outside the entrance until Luke and Gretchen cleared the way. When they exited the enchanted cave, they looped back around to Valley View platform where they lingered, reluctant to depart.

Luke said, "I hope my ears stay young so I can still hear Willy next season."

"Me too, and I'm touched that he gave me my own bell," said Gretchen.

Both knew it was time to go. On their walk from Mount Haycock, Luke reached for Gretchen's hand. They would say many good byes today: to their friends, to familiar rock wonders of the glacial age, to the meandering paths and trails, to the strange and silly wildlife.

"I hope you have a good semester," Luke offered as they stopped to watch ducks swim in the pond.

"Ditto," Gretchen responded. "I've been thinking I'd like to take a class in anthropology."

Luke confided, "I'm seriously considering picking up another major, in environmental studies."

"I like it," replied Gretchen with a smile. "This summer has changed us."

They continued their walk in silence, listening to wind rustling leaves, chattering of squirrels, chirping of birds, an occasional quacking of a duck. Large gray clouds swept across the sky. When they reached Main Lodge, Bob approached to say his goodbyes. Gretchen hugged Bob and Dean and walked a short distance away, waiting for Luke.

Bob pulled Luke aside and whispered something in his ear. Gretchen watched from across the lodge and thought it was odd.

Dean said, "You rock!" and they pounded fists. Luke pulled him in for a bear hug and thanked him for another great season.

Walking to the parking lot, Gretchen asked what Bob had whispered.

Luke stopped and looked back at the park and then turned to Gretchen with a puzzled expression. "He told me not to worry. Said he'd take good care of *all* the creatures in the park, with strong emphasis on the word all."

"Do you think he knows about Willy?"

"Sure sounded that way," Luke admitted.

When they got to Gretchen's car, Luke hugged her and reminded her to keep in touch. Gretchen looked into his eyes with an unspoken wish for a kiss at the same moment Luke gently pressed his lips to hers. In that instant, both felt the promise of commitment and a vision of their future together. Gretchen returned a playful, affectionate smile, and pulled Luke to her for another, longer kiss.

The fluttering tingle, the precious spark of humanity and love, passed between them. Luke stood grinning as she drove away with her good-natured smirk and enthusiastic wave. She would probably text him before the day ended. If not, he would text her.

Luke looked up to Hawk's Cliff and whispered another good-bye to Willy. He was bothered by the abrupt end to their last meeting and reached for the bell around his neck.

He rang it, ever surprised at the gentle peal of the slim rod hitting its sides, comforted to have it with him. The bell was a cherished token of friendship and a reminder of his magical summer.

He heard the call of a chickadee, a favorite bird of his. It was cute, noisy, small and often hard to spot. Pulling field glasses from his car, he looked in the direction of the birdsong. No luck. It hid somewhere amid full branches of leaves.

He peered above the granite veins of pegmatite on Mount Haycock, still curious about the windmill Willy said was there. There was no sign of it, but what he did see made him pause and adjust the focus on his binoculars. Dotting the top of the cliff were a row of sparkling light glows.

The End